I0552345

Distorted by Time

Murray Watson

The world as we know it is a tangled profusion of events.
Michel Foucault

Contemporary history has created a new kind of human being – the kind that are put in concentration camps by their enemies and internment camps by their friends.
Hannah Arendt

Teviotdale

2025

Grosvenor House
Publishing Limited

The right of Murray Watson to be identified as the author of this
work has been asserted in accordance with Section 78
of the Copyright, Designs and Patents Act 1988

The book cover is copyright to Murray Watson

This book is published by
Grosvenor House Publishing Ltd
Link House
140 The Broadway, Tolworth, Surrey, KT6 7HT.
www.grosvenorhousepublishing.co.uk

This book is a work of fiction. Any resemblance to
people or events, past or present, is purely coincidental.

A CIP record for this book
is available from the British Library

ISBN 978-1-83615-142-5

Dedicated to the memory of my great, great uncle, James Watson (1836-1898), a four-times published author, whose most famous work was *Jedburgh Abbey and the Abbeys of Teviotdale*. This book was first published in 1877, revised in 1894 and reprinted in 2016. James Watson was also a poet:

About our little cottage in Teviotdale

Why dost thou, little painted flower,
Love to adorn our cot alone ?
Or bloom beneath the wintry shower,
When thy companions all are gone ?
Wouldst thou not rather fade away
Till wintry blasts and rains are o'er,
And come again with flowery May
To deck our little cottage door ?

Chapters

The Characters

Classmates

Robert Scott: The leader of the gang
Jimmy McCartney: A rogue and Roman Catholic
Bobby Elliot: A victim of polio
Kathleen Solomon: English-born and of the Jewish faith

The PoW

Gërnot Hersinger: Held in Stobs camp except when he was farm labouring

The McLeods

Mr McLeod: A sheep farmer
Mrs McLeod: The farmer's wife
Shona McLeod: Daughter
Gerry Singer: Formerly Gërnot Hersinger, a labourer

The Carluccis

Antonio Carlucci: An Italian immigrant pedlar
Gina Carlucci: Antonio's wife
Pietro Carlucci: Son
Bianca Carlucci: Daughter

The Singers - 1st generation

Gerry: Formerly Gërnot Hersinger, Husband
Shona (née McLeod): Wife of Gerry
Hughie: Son

The Singers - 2nd generation

Hughie: Husband
Bianca (née Carlucci): Wife
Rory: Son

The Singers - 3rd generation

Rory: Husband
Kathleen (née Solomon): Wife

Others

Claudio Houde, A Canadian internee and terrorist. Paddy O'Rourke, a Fenian. Inspector McClintock, RCMP. Anne Field, civil servant. Mark Sinclair, student. Lorna Smyth, student. Dr Tom Drake, lecturer. The following real individuals make fictionalised appearances: Emily Hobhouse, T.C. Smout, The Earl of Athlone, Sir Alexander Clutterbuck, David Steel MP and Enoch Powell MP.

Chapter 1   Robert

1954 - Hawick

My mother pushed me out of the back door. I was not wearing my tackety boots. Earlier I had popped out to bring in the milk to find an erect column of cream forcing the silver bottle-top skywards. The glistening frost on the doorstep told me that I would not be able to engage in my latest hobby of scuffing the steel studs on the soles of my boots to leave a discharge of explosive sparks in my wake.

'Now don't you call in on that Jimmy McCartney on your way to school', were my mother's parting words. Mum had a pathological dislike of the McCartney family. She said Jimmy was common because he wore a balaclava under his school cap. And he never cleaned his boots. I later found out it was probably because Mr McCartney had spent time for fraud in Saughton Prison.

Jimmy had got me into serious trouble the week before and my dad gave me a real sore skelping when he returned from his shift in the mill. On my way home from school Jimmy and I had to cross the Waverley Line, which ran all the way from Edinburgh to Carlisle. It was a great place to play. Last Saturday, when we went to the morning kids' matinee at the Piv, we saw our favourite western, Hopalong Cassidy. Hopalong and his posse were involved in tracking down a group of bandits who had held up a train. The robbers had cunningly lain in wait round a bend in the track where they had placed a giant log to derail the train. To make sure they were ready in time, one of the bandits had knelt down on the track and put his ear to the rail to listen for the advancing locomotive.

Jimmy and I thought this was a beezer idea and we both lay down on the Waverley Line. When we heard a train approaching we rushed to a nearby bridge. We climbed up on the stone parapet to watch the train rushing by – belching smoke and that special smell of coal, oil, steam and sulphurous oxide that was unique to British Rail steam engines. When I got home there was a furious row. My face, hair, cap and blazer were covered in specs and blobs of soot. What made it worse was I had a black line of the track running across my cheek from ear to chin.

With my mother's instructions ringing in my ears I shuffled along Rinkvale Gardens dragging my school bag in the frost and made my way to Jimmy's in the Terraces. After picking him up we made our way to the third and fourth members of our wee gang. Bobby Elliot was a polio victim and was usually two steps behind, his progress being hindered by the clanking calliper on his left leg. In spite of his disability Bobby was a feisty character. His dad was a shepherd, who often took Bobby with him trudging through tussocky fields, up and down steep hills to check if the ewes were lying on their backs. On one occasion Bobby ended up having a fierce fight with his big brother over who should be first on the shoogly bridge over the Fenwick Burn. The fight came to an abrupt end when

Bobby took off his calliper and used it as a cudgel to hit his brother on the head.

The other member of our gang was a girl. Kathleen Solomon lived next to the school and we did not have much of a chance to say more than hello as she disappeared through the girls' gate into her half of the playground. Kathleen's father owned the local garage, Cole and Brydon. Unlike us, her family were rich. They owned a car, an Austin Seven, and the only television set for miles. Kathleen was a tomboy, who I later remembered as a very pretty girl with strawberry blonde straight hair framing an oval porcelain face, gentle pink cheeks and an elegant nose that was neither too short or too long. Mum didn't like her either. She said Kathleen was a Jew; but I didn't know what that meant.

Kathleen was also English. That confused me because at school we were taught to hate the English, and I liked Kathleen. History lessons were all about our hero, Robert the Bruce, who defeated the English king's much larger army at Bannockburn. In music lessons we sang, *'Sons of heroes slain at Flodden'*. We rehearsed it over and over again so it was perfect for the Cornet's annual visit to the school. Every year the Cornet came and reminded us that over four hundred years ago boys, only a little older than us, had routed a troop of English soldiers outside the town. The English soldiers' crime was that they they had slain the boys' fathers, older brothers and uncles at the Battle of Flodden. The young lads stole the English flag and every year since the battle it was paraded round the town by the Cornet and his followers on horseback. Even at home I was taught to hate the English. At the start of every English rugby season my father would regale us with the story of how he and a group of his teenage friends from the High School travelled by train in 1938 through some strange-named towns like Carlisle, Carnforth, Crewe and Gerrards Cross to go to Twickenham to watch Scotland trounce England to win the Calcutta Cup and Triple Crown. Dad also never failed to mention that if it hadn't been for the war he probably would have been selected to play for Scotland. He was, I was told, quite good but whether he was that good we will never know.

My problem was that I liked Kathleen. She looked like us. She behaved like us. But, she didn't sound like us. Her accent reminded me of the plummy *BBC Home Service* tones of Daphne Oxenford, who I used to listen to every day on *Listen With Mother*. My state of confusion was added to at school. We were encouraged to be proud to be British. After all we had defeated the Hun and we always stood for the national anthem at the end of the Saturday morning kiddies' film show. What was the difference between British and English and can the English be Jews? It was a mystery to me. I suppose I summed up my confusion in the way I wrote my name and address in my jotter: Robert Walter Scott, 1 Minto View, Hawick, Roxburghshire, Scotland, Great Britain, United Kingdom, British Isles, Europe, Western Hemisphere, Planet Earth, The Universe.

After we arrived at school we didn't have long in the playground before the bell went and we all rushed to stand in queues. I was in the primary 6 boys' queue and we lined up next to the girls who were not supposed to talk to us, but they did. Mrs McNab, the headmistress, caught one of the girls talking and made both primary 6 queues stand still and silent for five minutes while the other classes filed in. It was freezing and we were all shivering when we shuffled into the classroom.

It was warm inside, with a hint of the smell of sour milk. For some strange reason our teacher, Miss Broatch, kept the crate of the small bottles of milk we got at break on a shelf above the cast iron radiator. By the time we came to drink the milk the cream at the top had turned a pale shade of greeny white.

We all sat at small wooden desks with ink wells half full of blue black Quink. A pencil and pen with a nib, usually bent or broken, lay in a runnel at the top of the desk. Jimmy sat at the front next to a cupboard with a large conical dunce's cap sitting on the top, ready to be given to anyone who made a mistake with the 'reading out loud'. Kathleen, Bobby and I sat in the back row. The walls were covered with large Bartholomews' world maps showing countries in red to remind us that the British Empire spanned the globe. Other pictures showed hedgehogs, rabbits, robins, spiders, oak trees and the kings and queens of England and Scotland. There was a hubbub from the babble of conversation combined with the teeth-tingling noise of wooden chair legs being scraped across the ink-stained parquet floor.

There was a sudden silence. Miss Broach had come through the door.

'Good morning primary 6'.

'Good morning Miss Broatch'.

'Be seated.'

There was renewed scraping of wooden chair legs. Miss Broatch stood behind her table, which was on a raised dais in front of the blackboard covered in a layer of chalk dust rather like the hoar frost outside. In her chilly voice Miss Broatch said. 'all the girls stand up. We are going to do our seven times table. After me:

Seven ones are seven
Seven twos are fourteen
Seven threes are twenty one
Seven fours are twenty eight'.

The girls repeated the seven times table all the way up to 'seven twelves are eighty four'.

'You can sit down now girls. Now it is the boys turn. Stand'. More shuffling of chairs as the girls sat and the boys stood. 'Now boys recite the eight times table.' This rote learning went on for some minutes until it came to the twelve times table when both boys and girls had to stand and say it together.

Miss Broatch then tested individuals firing questions at random. 'Solomon what are five fives'? 'Twenty five Miss.' 'Elliot what's nine eights'? Bobby took a few seconds to get to his feet. 'Seventy two Miss'. The teacher asked half a dozen other pupils and looking somewhat disappointed at not catching anyone out said, 'now we are going to do a spelling test. McCartney spell liaison'. Jimmy went red in the face and slowly got to his feet. 'L. E. E. . . . Can I start again? L. I. A. S. O. N.' He sat down.

'Stand. Come out to the front'. Miss Broatch reached into her desk drawer and brought out a two foot six long tawse. The leather belt was split into two at one end. 'That is not how you spell liaison'. She rolled back one half of the split end of the belt. 'Hold out your hand. I am going to teach you how to spell'. She spat out, 'L. I. A. I. S. O. N.'. With an emphasis on the second "I" she brought down the belt on Jimmy's hand with a vicious twist of her wrist. Jimmy had experienced this pain and humiliation before. He was determined not to cry and bit the inside of his lip drawing blood leaving a sharp metallic taste in his mouth. Miss Broatch secretly hoped Jimmy would blub in front of his class mates. She continued, 'I am going to ask you to spell liaison again at the end of the week and if you get it wrong again I am going to give you the other half of the belt . . . twice'. At that the bell went and the milk monitors sprang into action and distributed the evil smelling curdling brew.

Playtime.

The boys went to the left, the girls to the right, separated by a four foot six high stone wall. Jimmy was still hurting. His left hand was stinging in agony and a red weal was spreading up the inside of his arm. We knew that teachers were told only to belt the hand and to avoid the arm. But Miss Broatch was a sadist. Normally we would have torn off our blazers and used them as goalposts for a game of playground footie. But this morning was different.

Jimmy said, 'this morning we are going, we are going to have a pissing competition'.

I knew what was coming.

The teachers, like the pupils, had to use outdoor lavs and the ladies' cubicle was just behind the four foot six high wall. We positioned ourselves a couple of feet from the wall, undid the buttons on our flies, fumbled inside the slit of our Y-Fronts, pulled them out and pointed skywards. When we heard Miss Broatch coming, we could see her red hair over the wall striding towards the door of the ladies' lav, Jimmy said, one, two, three . . . fire. We all released our by-then bursting bladders. Bobby barely reached half way up the wall and mine only got as high as the coping. Jimmy produced an amazing parabola that soared above the wall.

There was a shriek.

'Direct hit', retorted a smiling Jimmy.

*   *   *

The bell went to signal the end of break. The girls ran to the left and the boys to the right to form orderly queues. As usual Bobby brought up the rear. We had to wait a little longer than usual for Miss Broatch to return to the classroom. And when she did she was wearing a worn brown tweed jacket with leather patches on the elbows rather than the smart twin set she had on at the beginning of the morning.

'Right children. Open your desks and take out your knitting needles. Remember it is plain one, purl one, plain one, purl one'.

Hawick was the knitwear capital of Scotland, if not the world, so there was no stigma whatsoever for the boys to learn how to knit. After all it was the men who were the frame workers producing the garments, with the women relegated to more menial tasks such as collar linking or greasy mending. In primary 4 we had learned how to crochet using a crochet hook to do yarn over stitches to make a mat on which to place our tea pot. I was very proud that this was used every day at home to protect the kitchen table. This year we were knitting a protective square glove to lift a boiling kettle off the trivet by the fire. I was not very good at knitting, dropping so many stitches that the finished item looked like a poorly designed piece of lace. I also could not cast on or cast off and needed Miss Broatch's help.

We sat for half an hour clicking our needles and trying to pick up dropped stitches. It was still a while to go before the lunch break when Miss Broatch said, 'take out your history jotters'. History was my favourite subject.

'Today I am going to tell you about David Livingstone, a famous Scottish explorer and missionary. He went to darkest Africa navigating the Limpopo River and discovering some giant waterfalls which he named in honour of our great Queen Victoria. While he was there he was attacked by a vicious lion which he fought off, even though he had a badly mauled arm'.

After a pause, she resumed, 'while I tell you about how Dr Livingstone civilised the natives and converted them to believe in Jesus I want you to draw a picture of Livingstone fighting the lion'. The rest of the lesson flew by and then it was time for lunch. The afternoon too was a blur because this was Friday. My mind was focussed on our Friday afternoon ritual. At the end of every week Bobby, Jimmy, Kathleen and I would go to our gang hut next to the railway line. We weren't really a gang but we liked to think that our gang hut, a bombed out signal box, was our special, secret place. We discovered it when we were in P2. Almost hidden by tall purple willow herb the former signal box had suffered a direct hit from one of the Luftwaffe's bombers in the last days of the war.

The signal box remained hidden by willow herb especially at the end of summer but for most of the year it was difficult to see, being concealed by a profusion of elder saplings. The brick walls, or what remained of them were between three and four feet high. There was no roof, no door or windows and the floor, when you pulled back the weeds, was covered with broken glass. In one corner the only remains were a rusty metal box where the signalman kept the detonators he used to place on the line as a warning to engine drivers when it was too foggy to see the signals. One day we managed to open the box and were disappointed to find there were no explosives inside. It did, however, make an excellent storage box for our games. We had built up a fantastic collection of bools, aggies, cats' eyes, cork screws, devils' eyes, onion skins and my favourite, a muckle big shooter, which began life as a ball bearing. There was also a bag of jacks containing a bouncy rubber ball and a load of metal jacks that looked like miniature tank traps. The aim of the game was to pick up the largest number of scattered jacks when the bouncing ball was in the air.

When we arrived in the gang hut we formed a circle and sang, or to be more accurate intoned, our ceremonial anthem:

Hitler has only got one ball,
Göering has two but very small.
Himmler is rather sim'lar,
But poor old Goebbels has no balls at all.

We boys were all Wolf Cubs and Kathleen was a Brownie. As Cubs we all had sheath knives which we kept in our school bags. Kathleen did not have a knife. This particular Friday we decide to play targets. There was a trunk of an old gnarled elder tree protruding through one of the walls of the signal box. We had carved a target on the old tree somewhat between a dartboard and archery target. In turn we took our knives out of their leather sheaths - Kathleen had to borrow one. Standing with our backs to the far wall each of us, in turn, held the sharp pointed knife by the tip and raised it up to shoulder height, before hurling it at the target. The aim was to get nearest to the Bull's Eye. There was a forfeit for the person who was furthest away. This week Kathleen was furthest away. That was strange because it was usually Bobby. Kathleen's forfeit was being made to stand to attention while the other three got to throw their knives into the ground with the ultimate winner being the one whose knife landed closest to her feet. Strangely we never missed and no blood was ever spilt. This time was no different but, with Jimmy's knife bouncing off Kathleen's Start-Rite sandals, she decided to get her own back.

A nervous and relieved Kathleen announced, 'it's my turn now. We are going to play doctors and nurses and examine each other'. We had played this game once before and the only person that appeared to enjoy it was Kathleen, the nurse. 'I'll start as the first patient and you can examine me'. Before we had time to experience a sense of nervous tension in the pits of our stomachs Kathleen raised her skirt to reveal a pair of voluminous navy blue knickers. The blood rose to my cheeks and I feared I must have resembled the stop light at the town's only set of traffic lights. She then pulled her knickers down revealing two red circular weals where her knicker elastic had cut into her thighs. I had never been so close to a girls bits before and all we boys stood there transfixed. After what seemed like an age Kathleen said, 'I shall be nurse now. Drop your shorts'. We remained transfixed and Kathleen approached me, having pulled her knickers up. She slid her right hand up my shorts, fumbled with her fingers through the slit in my Y-fronts and gently squeezed.

'Oooooooooaaaaaaagh'

'You are different from my brother Samuel. He doesn't have that bit of wrinkly skin at the end'.

At that I had had enough and ran all the way home.

After that Fridays were never the same, that is until we were at the High School, but that is another story. Before the end of term, after learning more about Livingstone, Stanley and Mungo Park we decided to go exploring. Over the last few months we had found various bits of shrapnel near the gang hut and on one occasion found the spent case of a Lee Enfield 202 bullet. We were convinced that one day we would come across a UXB. No such luck, but we did find a small rusty tin that Jimmy needed to prize open with his sheath knife. There were two small items inside. One looked like an old military dog tag from the Great War. The other was a black medal in the shape of a Maltese cross. The medal had, on one side, a crown on top of the initial W and on the obverse was inscribed *FÜR KRIEGS-HILFSDIENST*. The tag was covered in mud and corrosion. After cleaning it up we could see what we thought might be the name of a battleship, SMS Weisbaden, a number (2736194) and a name that looked like *Deckoffizer* Gërnot Hersinger. We immediately realised that the *Deckoffizer* must have been a prisoner of war who had escaped from Stobs Camp, which had incarcerated some 6,000 PoWs, five miles south west of the town.

* * *

During the summer holidays we decided to find out more about Stobs Camp. It was up the Slitrig Valley where the road was relatively flat and good for cycling. Three of us had bikes and I had just got a new, second-hand red Raleigh with 26 inch wheels and three-speed Sturmey-Archer gears. Unfortunately Bobby could not ride a bike but after telling his auntie Jean that we wanted to find out more about an escaped PoW she said that there were lots of documents, photos and papers about Stobs in the basement of the Library where she worked.

So one sunny Tuesday morning during the school holidays Jimmy, Kathleen and I set off, with packed lunches in our saddlebags up the Newcastleton Road, past Turnbull the Dyers and the English Church before we reached the countryside. Bobby headed off, hobbling to the Library. None of us had been out of the town this way before but as expected the fields were full of sheep. It was relatively easy going with the wind behind our backs until we arrived at the turn-off for Stobs just after three fields full of pigs. We were faced with a steep hill that wound forever upwards and under a giant viaduct which had been built as a link to the Waverley Line so that trains could transport PoWs, guards and provisions to the camp. We had to get off to push our bikes up the hill, constantly swatting flies that buzzed out of the huge banks of ferns at the roadside. Breathless, we arrived at the top with sweat dripping off our faces. An amazing sight greeted us. We were at the top of a hill overlooking a steep valley split by the Penchrise Burn. On the far side there were high wire-mesh fences topped by razor wire. Inside this ring of rusty steel there was a grid of roads bounding dozens of long wooden huts or what appeared to be foundations where wooden huts may once have stood. There was the odd brick building and a football pitch on top of the hill at the far side. Down at the burn there appeared to be what looked like an outdoor swimming pool and a dam. We later learned that the prisoners had dug an Olympic-size swimming pool diverting water from the burn and a dam that was used to generate electricity for the camp. The prisoners were an enterprising bunch. Through the guards they used to sell ornaments, carved from sheep bones, as well as surplus black bread produced in the camp bakery. Unlike the town there was no bread rationing and hungry locals were happy to buy bread from the prisoners, even though it was black.

We had no idea that Stobs was as big as this. Taking the number of PoWs and guards together Stobs had a larger population than nearby Jedburgh and Selkirk. We could not wait to get back and tell Bobby and to discover what he had found out at the library.

Earlier in the day Bobby went down O'Connell Street, to the High Street then along North Bridge Street, dragging his heavy calliper behind him. It was an exhausting and hot journey, made almost bearable by a sense of anticipation and by the friendly smiles and greetings he received from people he encountered on the street. Outside the Post Office he was nearly knocked over by the huge Bill Macfarlane. Macfarlane played in the second row for the town's rugby team and earlier in the season won his first cap for Scotland. 'Whoa Bobby, I didnae see you doon there. Are you okay'? Bobby was struck dumb. Macfarlane was one of his sporting heroes and though he went to watch him when the Hawick rugby team played at home Bobby had never spoken to any of the players, even Darcy Smith, another internationalist, who lived in the same close as the Elliot family.

The library, a splendid art deco building, a gift to the town from a Scots-born American philanthropist just before the Great War, was not far from the Post Office. When Billy arrived he was clearly in a pother and his auntie Jean sat him down and gave him a refreshing glass of Cremola Foam. Once he had recovered auntie Jean said, 'I'll take you down to the basement and show you what we've got'. She led him back out towards the front door and paused by a spiral staircase which had a chain bearing a sign saying STAFF ONLY. PUBLIC KEEP OUT. Bobby was a bit flummoxed when he saw that he could see down to the floor below through the narrow spiral stairs. Billy's leg would make the corkscrew twisted steps difficult to navigate and his vertigo didn't help either. Auntie Jean was aware of the problem and she gently held his hand and helped him descend. The basement was a dark musty place with a pervading aroma of damp, foxed paper. The place was lined with rows of metal shelves filled with sturdy archive boxes, a miscellany of documents, old newspapers, books and trade directories. At the far end there was an old, large, leather-topped Victorian desk with an antique banker's lamp with a green shade on it. 'Go and switch that desk light on and after I have shown you how to find stuff about Stobs you can sit in yon captain's chair and write up your notes'.

Near the desk there was a row of shelves with at least twenty boxes labelled 'Stobs Military Camp'. Billy could only carry two boxes at a time and after three trips there was no more room on the desk. He gingerly opened the first box and found a pile of old newspapers. The banner, in a big bold germanic type face, read: **Stobsiade**. The lead story began: *'So zieh denn, kleine "Stobsiade", Als erstes Exemplar ins Feld; Du findest, wie wir hoffen, Gnade In unsrer drahtgefassten Welt'*. Bobby quickly realised this made no sense to him and finding the next box full of **Stobsiade** newspapers moved on to the third box. That was full of official documents headed *KÜCHE, KRANKENHAUS, KLINIK, FRIEDHOF* and a whole host of other undecipherable words. Bobby soon found that all the other boxes only stored documents in German so he took them back to the shelves.

Having suffered from polio for the last eight years Bobby was not a person who gave up without a fight. He continued his search down the shelves and came across a group of boxes bearing the international Red Cross flag and the words Red Cross, Stobs Camp. He took two of these back to the desk. They were a bit heavier than the first boxes and Bobby felt hopeful. Opening the first he could see they were personal letters to prisoners, some parts redacted by the prison censor, from places like München, Heidelberg, Berlin and Grübenzeil. He couldn't understand any of them and close to tears he yelled. 'auntie Jean is there anything in English'?

After a few minutes he heard his auntie Jean's high heels clicking down the metal staircase. 'What's the matter wee Bobby'?

'All this stuff is in a foreign language and I can't understand it'.

'Give us a minute. I think there are documents in English over there'. They both moved across the basement and there were half a dozen or so boxes with red labels on the side. One said, Ministry of Defence; another Provisions; another PoWs Arriving by Rail and another Press Cuttings re. PoWs.

'That's the one I want', said Bobby grabbing the box and reading a smaller label that said *The Scotsman*, *Daily Mail*, the *Hawick Express* and *Southern Reporter*. Bobby was really excited about this find and rushed back to the large Victorian desk clutching his prize. Once inside the box he saw piles of faded press cuttings, some dated with the name of the newspaper scribbled on them and others more crumpled and torn.

The first cutting he pulled out was from the *Southern Reporter* dated 13th January 1916. It read: 'Carl Michalski, a German sailor aged 20, escaped from Prisoner of War Internment Camp at Stobs on 5th January. Dark complexion, eyes and hair and with a small black moustache. Wearing a military pattern greatcoat, a brown corduroy jacket and dark trousers'.

The second cutting was also from the *Southern Reporter* dated 2nd November 1916. It read: 'Three Prisoners of war escaped from Stobs Internment Camp on Friday night. All three were originally from sunk German cruiser Gneisenau at the Battle of the Falkland Islands. Two were recaptured at Rutherglen and the other at Spittal by Berwick. His name was Julius Schmidt, who knew the district well having come to Tweed Dock on ships in the wood-carrying trade. He had six shillings and "abundant food" in a "strong wooden box"'.

The third cutting was from the *Hawick Express* dated 18th October 1917. It read: 'Escape from Stobs.

FIVE HUNS AT LARGE. Five German prisoners of war, viz., Renhold Kraft, Julius Plizm, Paul Schultze, Wilhelf Borehunstani and George Giffers Hoomam, escaped from Stobs Camp on Wednesday night'. Bobby then found a cutting from the *Scotsman* dated 11th November 1915. It was a little different but still concerned escapees. It read: 'COURT-MARTIAL AT STOBS TRIAL OF TWO GERMAN PRISONERS. A military court was held at Stobs yesterday, at which they tried the German prisoners of war Gustav Beblein and Alfred Jokscli, who made their escape from Stobs Concentration Camp'. By now Bobby was getting a wee bit hungry. It was past tea time and he knew he was in for a row when he got home.

'What time do you think this is? Where on earth have you been? I have been worried stiff'. Mrs Elliot was not pleased. 'It's straight up the stairs for you and you're only getting bread and marge and a glass of water. And, you are grounded until tomorrow morning'.

Meanwhile I was just finishing a plate of mince and tatties with some rather mushy and salty carrots. I stifled a belch in my hankie and said, 'Mum. I am off out'.

'You're no long in. Where are you off to now'?

I couldn't wait to hear what Bobby had found out at the library and to tell him all about our day at Stobs Camp. I made my way down the street and l knocked on the Elliots' door. After what seemed like an age Mrs Elliot opened it.

'Hello,' I said. 'Can Bobby come out to play'?

'No he cannot. He's in disgrace and grounded until tomorrow'.

My enthusiasm was punctured. *What's he done now?* I know Mrs Elliot can sometimes go over the top but generally speaking she is very sympathetic towards Bobby's problems. I wondered what he had done to make her so cross.

The following day the four of us met up at the street corner just in time to see the milkman's horse do a big steaming dump in the middle of the road. Jimmy ran home and returned with a shovel for his papa's roses. That turned out to be a piece of good fortune because papa McCartney had been a midshipman during the Great War and there was nothing he liked more than to regale us with tales about his exploits at the Battle of Jutland. We could ask him what he knew about the German sailor's identification tag and medal we found. I rushed home to get the rusty tin box and we headed off to papa McCartney's house.

We found him in the garden dead-heading his roses. He was very pleased with the present we had brought. He pulled out a flask of tea and sat down on a rickety wooden bench. 'I can see you have something else to show me. What is it'?

We all began talking at once.

'Wheesht. One at a time'.

Once again we all started talking at the same time. Papa McCartney said, 'Kathleen you start',

'Well just before the end of term we played a game of explorers seeing what we could find along the railway line near the old bombed out signal box. Earlier in the year we had found bits of shrapnel and spent bullet cases. This particular day we found a rusty tin box with what we thought was a German sailor's identification tag and medal inside. We thought it might have belonged to an escaped PoW and yesterday three of us cycled to Stobs Camp and Bobby went rummaging through old documents in the library. We can't wait to discover what he found out'.

'Let me see the box' said papa McCartney. 'Well, I can confirm that the tag and the medal belonged to a German sailor, and I can tell you a bit more about him. But first, Bobby what did you find out at the library'?

'A lot of the papers were in German so I couldn't understand them but my auntie Jean found me some boxes that contained documents in English. What they told me was that Stobs was a very large camp housing five or six thousand German soldiers and sailors. I don't think conditions could have been very good because the *Scotsman* newspaper called it a concentration camp. There were a lot of press cuttings about escaped prisoners and most seem to have been recaptured and I wondered if our German sailor had escaped and been recaptured or perhaps shot in Hawick. I only had time to go through a few of the press cuttings and I did not find one with the name of our German sailor. I think that we should all go back and look through the cuttings to see if we can find him'.

'That's really interesting,' said papa McCartney. 'Let me have a look at the box'. He picked out the medal twirled it round in his hand, scratched his head and said, 'I think that's a Merit Cross for War Aid. If it belonged to our German sailor he was a brave man'. The old man turned to examine the identification tag. 'This tells us a lot. See here this was his ship, SMS Wiesbaden. The Wiesbaden was a light cruiser and I was on HMS Invincible that sank her at the infamous Battle of Jutland in 1916 or was it 1915? My God that was a fierce fight. The sound of the guns was deafening, the ship juddered and vibrated every time the guns went off and I can still smell the smoke and the cordite. The firing went on for hours and it took a long time for the Wiesbaden to go down. I thought all their crew were killed or drowned. I don't think we picked anyone up out of the briny though with you finding this tag it indicates there must have been at least one survivor'.

'Amaaaazing,' exclaimed Jimmy and Bobby simultaneously.

'Go on', encouraged Kathleen. 'What else can you tell us'?

'Well, his rank was *Deckoffizer*. He was about the same level as I was in the ship's pecking order. His name was Gërnot Hersinger. I am sure the number must tell us something too but I don't know what. I can tell you though that the identification tag was issued by the German Imperial Navy. We had tags too as members of His Majesty's Royal Navy. Someone once told me that the Germans introduced the idea in the Franco-Prussian War and called them *Hundemarken*. Apparently the Kaiser didn't like the idea of calling his soldiers dogs so they changed the name to identification tags. We still call them dog tags'.

Fortunately for us Mr McCartney Senior was a bit of a history buff. He was a high heid yin in the Hawick Archaeological Society and editor of their annual transactions. Unknown to us, last year he had written an article about how Stobs had been used as an internment camp for enemy aliens and as a training camp for the KOSBs and the Coldstream Guards during the last war. Apparently the surrounding moorland and hills made it the perfect location for field manoeuvres and artillery practice. After the war the camp was largely dismantled and many of the wooden huts that had housed PoWs and soldiers had been sold off to local farmers to house livestock and sundry agricultural machinery.

'We need to go back to the library and do some more research to find out all we can about *Deckoffizer* Hersinger' continued papa McCartney. 'Bobby you told us there were boxes and boxes of press cuttings about escaped prisoners. As you found our German's tin box six miles away in Hawick he must have escaped and lost it near the railway line and the old signal box'.

The following day the four of us and papa McCartney trooped off to the library. Bobby's auntie Jean was surprised when asked for her help again but being the helpful old cove she was she went and got the key to open the door to the basement. With five of us we had a box each and after a couple of hours we had trawled through all the cuttings and listed the names of all the prisoners. There were loads but no one with the name of our German sailor.

We were a bit despondent but papa McCartney said that during the war there was press censorship and not every escape would have been reported in newspapers. During our hunt, however, we did discover that quite a number of the PoWs were German sailors, with dozens of them losing their ships during the Battle of Jutland.

Chapter 2   Gërnot

1918 - Stobs Camp & South Africa

Deckoffizer Gërnot Hersinger was feeling especially sorry for himself. It was his nineteenth birthday and there he was sitting in a very cold, bare cell in solitary confinement after he was caught escaping from Stobs Camp.

Only the day before he got the taste of freedom. He had been part of a work party helping to load a flock of sheep on to a train at Stobs Halt. The sheep were bound for slaughter at a nearby abattoir. At one point the flock broke into three groups. One of the sheep dogs went haring off after a dozen or so ewes heading in the direction of the piggery at the bottom of the hill. The sheep and dogs were followed by four of the other prisoners in the working party. The two armed guards brought up the rear leaving me with the sheep that had already been loaded on to the livestock wagon. That left me on my own and sensing the opportunity to escape undetected in the chaos, I hid myself on the floor amongst a forest of woolly legs, sheep shit and urine. My luck was in and twenty minutes or so later I heard the steam engine chuffing away pulling out of the Halt.

I realised that I would soon be missed. Stobs was in the middle of nowhere surrounded by desolate moorland with only the occasional sheep for company.

This environment did not make escaping easy and most attempts to get away involved hiding on a train and travelling north to Edinburgh or south to Carlisle. Going north was the favoured direction because that was towards the east coast. Most of the PoWs dreamt of stealing a sailing boat at places like Berwick on Tweed or Seahouses or contacting a U-Boat that allegedly waited off the coast to pick up escaped prisoners and take them home.

Fearing a reception committee further up the line I decided to jump off the train at the nearby town of Hawick. That was a big mistake. There were three policemen and one armed soldier on the platform. I ran and tripped over a pile of coal next to the signal box. The small bag that carried my rations for lunch and the precious box that had my medal and identification tag in it went flying. My English was not very good but I could understand the gruff command, 'hands up you Hun'. I was well and truly recaptured.

Sitting here huddled under my great coat it really was cold and logs for the small stove were rationed as part of the punishment for going AWOL. In any event the logs, which had been left out in the snow, were so wet that they gave out little heat and lots of smoke. I kept going over in my mind the mistake I made by being an opportunist and not carefully planning my escape. I knew there was an escape committee and I feared that the *Oberst* would make life more difficult for me than Captain Gray, the camp commandant, for my failure to consult the committee about my escape plans. But then there had been no plans. I found myself outside the wire and the guards' attention had been distracted by escaping sheep and out-of-control dogs. I took my chance and paid for it.

The guys in my hut, Hut 57, had often talked about how not to go mad if we ever found ourselves in solitary so, in a sense, I was prepared. Before the war Hans Blick had taught physical education in a gymnasium. He suggested that members of the military try to keep their bodies and minds fit. He introduced calisthenics, a form of exercise that used an individual's body weight as a form of resistance. He said that these methods had originally been used by the armies of Alexander the Great and the Spartans at the Battle of Thermopylae. We practiced these in the hut. The only bit of equipment we needed were the exposed rafters to perform chin-ups and pull-ups. Other than that we only needed space to do press-ups, squats, handstands and leg raises. Fortunately there was just enough space and rafters in solitary to perform all these exercises.

We also talked about trying to remain positive by thinking about happy memories and events in the past. Just thinking about what I needed to do made me feel a lot better about the depressing situation I found myself in and to stop thinking that I was a failure for getting caught so easily.

It was not long, however, before I started having negative thoughts. I tried calisthenics but after doing nineteen squats I felt a painful tug in my calf muscle and had to stop. Still, determined to be positive, I started to recall happy memories. But I could only remember unhappy ones. I remember being told I was born in a British concentration camp in Pietersburg in Northern Transvaal, South Africa. Delving into the depths of my mind I remembered our family story. My father Helmut and his brother Jurgen had both been farmers, who lost their business, when the French defeated us at the Battle of Saarbrücken some fifty years ago. The family decided to emigrate. Jurgen went to the German colony of Rwanda and my dad and his young wife travelled to Northern Transvaal near the mountainous Zoutpansberg region. The land was fairly flat where they settled and they, I understand from listening to family stories in my early teens, made a success of their new agricultural business. They got on well with their Boer neighbours. The Boers, many of whom spoke German, made their money from lumber and from the capture and sale of black children as apprentices to Boer farmers.

I was told that all was not sweetness and light. There was a considerable amount of hatred and hostility that marked Boer relations with local black tribes. What made matters worse was that a Cape Colony renegade, Coenrad Buys, married into a local black family. His mixed marriage introduced an extra layer of tension into local relationships between the races.

In spite of this evident atmosphere of unpleasantness the family enjoyed their new life. We found the veldt an extraordinarily beautiful place and so different from the lands around the River Rhine where we came from. In Transvaal the vegetation was luxuriant, the land fertile, as well as the strange trees with a maze of creepers at their foot. My mother never ceased to be amazed by the views that stretched as far as the eye could see, the big skies and the stunning sunsets. Dad enjoyed visiting native kraals and once he became accustomed to the men wearing strange headdresses and bearing spears and shields managed to sell his excess produce to the natives. The noises and smells were different too - irritating mosquitoes incessantly whining in your ears at night complementing the occasional roaring lions and trumpeting elephants bringing sleep to an end. Apparently it took a few years for my parents to become used to this night time cacophony.

The stories told to me as a child painted an idyllic life which came abruptly to an end with the outbreak of the Boer War. Years of hostility, suspicion and jealousy involving the British, the Dutch and a host of native tribes - Zulus, Kaffirs, Hottentots, Bushmen and Bantus - erupted into a very bitter and cruel conflict. It was the usual story. England, the great colonial power wanted to unite the South African territories under their Union flag whereas the Boers and the Afrikaans-speaking farmers wanted to maintain their independence. Queen Victoria's army was militarily stronger but the troops were stung time and again by the Boers' guerrilla tactics. As Germans we weren't really involved in the conflict but we were seen by the British as Johnny Foreigner. In any case our natural inclination was to favour the Dutch.

The British army adopted a scorched earth policy to drive their enemies off the land and as an extra disincentive the Conservative government in London adopted the new policy of establishing concentration camps, to intern their enemies, black and white. The policy was to make the camps especially unpleasant and cruel places to live. Our family suffered from the Brits' scorched earth tactics. My father and mother, who was heavily pregnant with me, ended up in the Pietersburg camp near our burnt out farm in Northern Transvaal. In my short life Stobs was my second British concentration camp.

It was day ten of my time in solitary. I was beginning to get a bit depressed. My memory was playing tricks, not helped by remembering what I was told about the time when I was a baby and toddler in the Pietersburg concentration camp. My mother remembered a visit from Emily Hobhouse, a campaigner, who drew attention to the cruel and appalling conditions in the camps. Apparently she argued the camps were part of the English policy of extermination directed against the Boer population.

From my early memories and my Mum's stories Miss Hobhouse was right. There were about 2,000 people living in the camp, many of whom were ill with fever, measles and malaria. As a child I caught the measles and then developed double pneumonia and could count myself fortunate that I did not die like almost half of the inmates. We lived in overcrowded wagons surrounded by block houses. Latrines were few and far between, and they stank. There were no wells and water had to be brought in. On one occasion when there was an outbreak of scurvy I remember being given a beaker of lime juice - it was delicious. But life was hard. It was tough and in some respects prepared me for my time in Stobs, which was not as cruel, but was almost as harsh.

The Boer War came to an end in May 1902 and by the end of the summer the camp was disbanded and we were sent home. That was a shock. The English soldiers had torched the farmstead and all the outbuildings and the stock had totally disappeared, no doubt butchered to feed the troops. Many of our family's friends found themselves in similar situations and had to rebuild their lives from nothing. Fortunately for us, my father had been a saver and had stashed a horde of Burgersponds and Kruger coins he had built up over the years. He was also an extremely suspicious man and had buried them to keep them safe from robbers or natives. When we got home he went over to the well with a shovel in his hand. He marched due south and after taking 33 spaces he started digging. 'Thank the Lord. They are safe', he muttered. In a louder more confident voice he said, 'we are going to get the hell out of here'. A couple of weeks later we began the long and arduous journey back to Germany where we set up a new home in Wilhelmshaven, the main port of the Hochseeflotte of the Imperial German Navy.

My 28 days in solitary at Stobs Camp eventually came to an end. I was immediately summoned to face *Oberst* Steiffel. 'What the fuck do you think you were playing at? Do you realise that by making an unapproved escape attempt - and what a fucking shambles that was - you have buggered up one of our most promising escape routes. The Limeys have reinforced the guards round Hawick Station and the great escape we had planned for the Kaiser's birthday has had to be cancelled'. The Oberst was not a happy man. I was put on jankers for a month. That experience turned out to be just as miserable as solitary.

The war dragged on in stalemate in the trenches along the Maginot Line. At long last an Armistice was signed but we had to wait a few months before release from Stobs. During my time as a PoW I had been working as a labourer and shepherd at the nearby Rubers Hill Farm on the Cavers Estate. The McLeod family had been quite friendly and provided me with an old woollen greatcoat to keep me warm. They also fed me occasionally and their oldest daughter Shona, who was a bit of a looker, used to stay and chat when she brought me mince and tatties or lentil soup for my lunch. After talking to Mr McLeod and getting permission from camp commandant, Captain Gray, it was agreed that, rather than repatriation to Wilhelmshaven, I could stay on as a temporary labourer in return for board and lodging and what they called cigarette money.

Chapter 3   Gerald

1919 - Hawick & Liddesdale

Life in the Border hills was very pleasant. The years passed quickly by in a natural rhythm, from tupping in the autumn, to lambing around Easter, to shearing once the Common Riding was over. The McLeods' farm was not far from Stobs, near the Williestruther reservoir and near the Mair where, once a year, the local men, known as Teries, followed their leader, who was called the Cornet, on horseback. The men sang an untranslatable *Teri Bus Ye Teri Odin*. The Cornet carried a flag that had been captured by local youths from a troop of English soldiers during one of the regular wars between England and Scotland in the olden days. I was told that the Cornet had ridden the so-called Marches with his followers every year since the locals routed the English near Hawick in 1514. There were long memories in these parts.

The locals, on the whole, were not too antagonistic towards me, especially after I had changed my name to Gerald Singer. I had learned some English at school in Germany and the very distinctive Hawick accent I adopted was not too dissimilar from German speech. I was also very fond of fishing and spent hours at Williestruther. The silence there, interrupted only by the sound of the wind in the trees or bleating sheep, or the calls of moorhens, mallards and little grebes, was a refuge and comfort. As well as catching the occasional trout or pike I made friends with a number of fishermen who introduced me to the local dark brown beer at the Angling Club in Hawick. I knew that I was accepted when they started calling me Jerry, without malice. They told me it was short for Gerald! At the Angling Club bar the talk was about three things: rugby, the one that got away and women. I didn't know very much about rugby or women but I had lots to say about the five pounder that broke my line in August 1921.

It wasn't long before Shona taught me about women. On the day I moved into my but-n-ben there was a knock on my door. 'Good afternoon Gërnot. My father tells me that you are going to live with us and work on the farm'. It was Shona. I had seen a quite a lot of her when she brought me lunch when I was a PoW working as a trustee looking after the sheep. She was a shy lass with a fresh complexion and shining, black shoulder-length hair. What I noticed most were her breasts, which jostled for my attention inside her blouse. Even more discombobulating was the fact that the top three buttons of her blouse were undone. This was my first lesson about women. Every time I looked down from the top of Rubers Hill Farm into the steep narrow valley to the burn below I could not help but think of the cleave in Shona's garb.

'*Ja. . . Entschuldige,* I mean yes'. I had never been as embarrassed or confused speaking to another person before, and never when I had passed the time with Shona when eating lunches during the war. I was surprised that I had used the informal German way of saying sorry to people with whom you are on familiar terms rather than the more formal, "*Entschuldigen Sie*". I don't suppose Shona noticed my *faux pas* but she could not have helped noticing my deep red blushes. My cheeks felt on fire.

That was my first time alone with Shona after I ceased being a PoW. After that she came to see me nearly every day. We tended to spend our time with Shona innocently helping me with my English. She brought a *New Testament* and Sir Walter Scott's *Guy Mannering* in place of a text book. Each Sunday she would walk about two miles with me to the church. We went to the English Episcopal Church and not the Presbyterian St Mary's Kirk which was only a little bit further away, in Hawick. I never understood why they went to the English Church. I suppose it was because it was nearer the farm.

One Sunday when Shona was suffering from a broken toe after one of the cows had trodden on her foot she decided to ride her small pony, Victoria. On our way back to the farm something spooked Victoria. The pie-bald pony whinnied and reared, and, although Shona was an experienced rider, she was thrown, hitting the ground next to a steep bank with a resounding thud. Victoria bolted. Shona screamed and promptly slid down the bank into the River Slitrig. The old song told how the *Slitrig danced doon the glen*. Today the water was flowing faster than usual. Fortunately the icy, cold water quickly revived Shona from her temporarily unconscious state. I jumped into the river after Shona and reached out to rescue her. The first thing I grabbed was one of her jostling breasts. I was discombobulated again, but this feeling of excited discomfort was short-lived. My main concern was to safely retrieve Shona from the river. I took off my warm Sunday-best tweed overcoat and put it round Shona's shoulders. My but-n-ben was nearby and I carried her there and then lit a fire with some bone-dry kindling and small logs. The fire soon generated some heat. I removed my coat from her shoulders and Shona started to unbutton her wet blouse and followed this by removing her slip. I could not take my eyes off her and did not hear Shona asking for a towel. She was obliged to walk over to the pulley and get one down.

*   *   *

Our relationship changed after that fateful sabbath day. Almost immediately Mr and Mrs McLeod became warmer and more friendly. They had always been politely welcoming and did not treat me as the enemy as did some of their neighbours, who were less than welcoming to their indentured PoW labour from the camp. After rescuing Shona I felt I almost became part of the family.

As well as working on the family farm Shona had a job as a greasy mender at Laings and Hendersons, one of the knitwear mills in the nearby town of Hawick. Laings had about 350 employees. There were a handful of male managers and frameworkers with the rest of the employees being mill girls. The mill was a noisy and dusty place with the women either reverting to sign language or shrieking at the tops of their voices to make themselves heard. There was a strong bond of camaraderie amongst the the mill girls. Laings organised sports and social clubs with Shona often turning out for the hockey team. During breaks the girls would congregate for a blether and a cigarette, exchanging gossip about the local talent and who they hoped to dance with at the local hop at the Town Hall every Saturday night.

Late one Saturday night when walking home to the farm from the dancing Shona started to sob.

'What's the matter'?

'Nothing'.

"Come on. What's the matter? What's bothering you'?

After what seemed like an age Shona said, 'it was Jessie and Nan'.

'What about Jessie and Nan'?

'They ridiculed me for going around with a Hun and said that you and your kind had killed their brother at Ypres. They even went as far as asking me to squeeze and twist your balls when we were in bed together. They did not believe me when I said we had not been to bed together and that I had never even touched your private parts'.

I was gob smacked and did not know what to say. I put my arm round her shoulders. At first Shona flinched but then lay her head on my shoulder and I felt her wet tears run down my neck. We walked and meandered meaninglessly in the general direction of the farm for about an hour. Reaching my cottage Shona asked if she could come in.

'Gerald, I would like to go to bed with you and I promise I will not hurt you'.

Our relationship changed again after that night. We were both assiduous churchgoers and attended the following day's communion with a sense of guilt and shame. We both believed it was a sin to have relations out of wedlock. I knew that Shona felt the same way as me and that what we both wanted was to spend the rest of our lives together. To do that would require Mr McLeod's permission and as friendly as he was I felt that he would not want his daughter to wed someone who had been known as Gërnot Hersinger. The McLeod family, like most local families had lost relatives during the recent world war and memories were long in these parts.

Fortunately Mr and Mrs McLeod did not seem to find out that Shona had spent the night with me. With our bodies pressed against each other and our arms and legs entwined we never got to sleep and when the dawn chorus started around four in the morning Shona got up with alarm and said, 'I must get into my own bed. My parents must never know about tonight'.

Shona was a pragmatist and not so headstrong as me. She realised that we had to be patient and chaste to bring her parents round. Life continued as normal. It was the time of year when the lambs had to be separated from their mothers and after I helped Mr McLeod and his dogs round up the ewes we had two nights of high pitched bleating from the lambs trying to communicate with the lower pitched baaing of the ewes at the opposite end of the farm.

I was ever so conscious of the noises or should I say silence of the moorland that surrounded Rubers Hill Farm. There was the near incessant shushing of the wind occasionally interrupted by the warbling of curlews, the peewits or lapwings, the mewing of buzzards and the guttural croaking of the occasional raven. On warm dry days I would lie down at dinner time on the tussocky grass with fragrances of wild thyme and cotton grass providing a heady atmosphere. With Shona working in the mill I spent weekdays dreaming of our future together. On Saturday I got a half day and sometimes I would share my piece with Shona down at the burn and in the afternoon wander down to the park to watch her playing hockey.

In addition to Hogmanay there were two other very special occasions that took place every year. The first of these was the Common Riding, but being a foreigner I never really got to grips with its mysterious traditions. The other event was the Laings and Hendersons work's outing. On the second Saturday every July Mr Laing and Mr Henderson hired a train pulling six carriages to take their staff, family and friends to spend the day at Portobello.

When we turned up at Hawick Station at half past seven in the morning there was already a large crowd with gurning babies competing with the shrieking of their older brothers and sisters running wild with their buckets and spades. There was an eager sense of anticipation and we could hear the puffing of the train engine as it made its way down past the sheep market and across the bridge over the River Teviot. There was a clattering and banging of carriage doors as over a hundred adults, children, grannies and grandads scrambled into the train. The guard's whistle could be heard over the hubbub, there was a jerk and we were off to Waverley Station in Edinburgh. I never made it that far during the war.

Once inside the train we made our way along the corridor until we found a compartment with two free seats. I slid the door open and we piled in with a great sense of expectation about the journey and the day ahead. I put Shona's bag and raincoat on the overhead rack and sat down to be greeted by one of the other passengers saying, 'you can't sit here'. I immediately recognised Jessie and Nan, Shona's antagonistic shop floor colleagues. They were with their young men. Both were large rugby players who played for the Hawick Trades.

'You heard what my lassie told you', threatened the taller of the two, a raw-boned second row forward who stood up, towering over Shona and I in a most menacing manner.

'Why can't we sit here'? I politely and somewhat nervously asked.

'Because you are a bloody Hun .. and you smell'.

Shona said, 'let's go'.

I was reluctant to leave. The war was over and I had been accepted into the local farming community. Common sense prevailed and after rescuing Shona's things from the rack we exited into the corridor. There were no seats anywhere and we spent the rest of the journey standing up, being buffeted from side to side as the train jolted along the track.

Less than three hours later we arrived at Portobello on the edge of the North Sea, where a few years before I had spent a couple of hours supported only by my life jacket waiting to to be rescued and made a prisoner of war. This was a much happier occasion. When we arrived Jessie and Nan together with their boyfriends, who had had already consumed several bottles of beer, made their way along the beach towards Leith. We went in the opposite direction towards Joppa.

The tide was out and although it was sunny there was a nip in the breeze coming off the Firth of Forth. We made our way to the edge of the water. I stopped and took off my socks and shoes and rolled up my Sunday-best flannels. Like most of the other men on the beach I had already tied four knots in the corners of my handkerchief and placed it on my head as protection from the sun. Much to my surprise Shona hitched up her frock and undid the clasps on her suspender belt to take off her nylon stockings. We went for a paddle. The rest of the day was a blur, eating candy floss, walking along the prom, watching kids build sandcastles and go on donkey rides. All too soon, after a fish supper served in the *Edinburgh Evening News,* it was back home to Hawick. Fortunately we did not come across Jessie or Nan, and we found a couple of free seats. We fell asleep with Shona's head resting on my shoulder. I woke up just before we pulled into Hawick Station; perhaps it was the smell of the sewage works alongside the track that interrupted my slumbers?

*   *   *

43

I really needed that break. The war had been over for a couple of years and I had been working really hard for Mr McLeod. Not only did I feel grateful to him for taking me on from Stobs but I wanted to impress him that I was a good bet as a future son in law. I had learned a lot about farming and as the years went by I knew that from mid July to the middle of August was the busiest time of the year. It was the clipping time. Every day started at four in the morning. We would go out with the dogs into the hills. It was often a wee bit misty and we were never sure whether we should wait at home for the sun to burn it off. In those days we had to walk everywhere and the dogs sometimes ran with gay abandon; at other times they would snarl and growl. Before setting off we went into Mrs McLeod's kitchen and had a breakfast of porridge, bacon, eggs and scones. Mrs McLeod believed that her men should never work on an empty stomach. At dinner time she or Shona, if she wasn't working at the mill, would bring us a full bowl of soup, meat and tatties at midday. Then if we were going on clipping into the evening, we would get what was called high tea, maybe salad and bread or scones or a loaf. Sometimes the neighbours or their sons who were on holiday from school would help. The wee boys would crog or catch the sheep and bring them to the men on stools where they would manually clip the fleece off the sheep. This was a fairly skilled job and you did not want to botch it as it would reduce the value of the wool when it came to market. It was hard work but enjoyable and the craic was invariably good. As well as clipping the hogs and ewes we had to mark all the lambs, to castrate the male lambs, and then dip all the sheep against flies and maggots.

The annual cycle began again in October when we started feeding the tups ready to put them out on the hill towards the end of November. There would be three tups to 100 ewes. That would be the right time for delivering lambs around Easter time. Over winter, when the days were shorter there was less to do but we had to walk miles over the hills to check the flock and to make sure none of the ewes were lying helplessly on their backs. We also had to supply extra feed if the snow lay particularly deep and the sheep could not easily get to the grass. It was cold and hard work. I only earned about £1 a week and my biggest expense was a pair of leather boots that I needed to tramp over the frozen moorland. Even though they cost the equivalent of the price of two lambs the boots were worth it. Mr McLeod gave me an old threadbare tweed coat and along with a balaclava from my days at Stobs I could be relatively warm in the coldest of conditions. One day when I returned from the hills I took my coat off. It was frozen solid and stood erect like a statue in front of the fire until the heat from the grate melted it into a heap of steaming wool.

Once the weather became warmer and the daffodils and primroses began to bloom the ewes started lambing. That meant spending most of our time out in the hills. If you were lucky you came on a ewe that was in trouble and needed a hand, if you were unlucky you could miss her and find her lying dead next day. I had never put my hand up the backside of a sheep before. That was not a skill needed in the Kaiser's navy. Fortunately, Mr McLeod was a patient teacher and I quickly became quite skilled helping ewes in difficulty.

The days were long and with Shona having to leave home before seven in the morning to walk four miles to the mill in Liddesdale Road and then not getting home until gone seven in the evening we barely saw each other. In the summer there were precious moments spent down by the burn watching the sunset while in winter we were obliged to tryst in the musky, dusty steading sharing the space with the hens and pigs. Saturday was our half day so we could spend the afternoon together and in the evening go dancing or watching the latest Hollywood blockbuster at the Piv. Sunday we had to ourselves but we had to share it with God.

Every Sunday I breakfasted in the McLeods' kitchen. The washed-pine round table was laid for a full breakfast. The big copper kettle steamed on the trivet fixed to the range which shone brightly thanks to Mrs McLeod's application of lamp black the night before. Mr McLeod had a big carver chair with a patina going back several generations. Directly in front, before him, was a large family bible and a brass bell. The first bell rung was for prayers, the second was for breakfast. Once we had washed down the last scone with a cup of strong tea, sweetened with a spoonful of Lyle's green treacle, Mrs McLeod and Shona attended to the washing up while Mr McLeod and I went out into the yard to check on the hens and pigs. Around half an hour later, in our Sunday best, we set off to the Episcopal Church. We were allowed to chat and laugh whereas our presbyterian neighbours were instructed to make their way to the Kirk in silence. Once in church Mr McLeod and I took off our hats and sat in our pew alongside the women who were sitting primly with their hands in their laps having transformed their hitherto happy, smiling faces into expressions reflecting sabbath solemnity.

The social side of the church life made attendance something to look forward to, especially on communion Sundays. Whole families would come from miles around - from Penchrise, North House, Southwell, Flex, Whitchesters and further afield. There would be extended families of Scotts and Elliots. One of the most colourful of characters was a Bobby Elliot an itinerant shepherd who lived in Hawick. Bobby always brought his dog to church. It was normally well behaved but on one occasion during a more robust than usual singing of one of Charles Wesley's hymns, *Christ the Lord is Risen Today*, the dog started howling which set off most of the babies in the church crying. There were several sets of discordant noises competing with the congregation's singing and the organist's playing. The minister held up his hand and two of the church wardens removed the collie and took him into the graveyard. Peace was restored. Everyone stood up and following the minister's guidance started reciting the *Lord's Prayer*.

On communion Sundays every pew was filled and some parishioners had to stand in the aisles. The service was a protracted one starting at 10.30 and sometimes going on until the middle of the afternoon. There were several tables for communion which followed the sermon from the pulpit. The Rev. McAlister was not one of the fire and brimstone variety but nevertheless he delivered his sermons, sometimes over-long, with a passion that held no time for sinners. Descending from the pulpit he gave us his blessing and the sacramental formalities came to an end. Before heading for home, bread, cheese and milk was served in the manse kitchen and the men folk were sometimes treated to a dram. The minister and the elders dined in the manse and sometimes on the Mondays some of the principal parishioners were invited to a sumptuous Monday dinner. I, and as far as I know the McLeods, were never on this exclusive invitation list.

By the time we got home and had our tea it was almost time to go to bed, especially on dark winter nights when we only had the fire and a few winter candles to give us light. We did not have gas lights and we did not have an electricity supply until 1936. Still, Sundays were good days because it was the only day when I could spend every hour with Shona. Although devoid of privacy we found it easy to press our thighs together on the pew while in full view of her parents.

*　*　*

I had been working for the McLeods for nearly four years. I had learned a lot about sheep farming and I think Mr McLeod considered me to be reliable and a hard worker. I also think they were aware that I was courting their daughter and with strains of my German

48

accent having morphed into broad Hawick I was generally accepted in the neighbourhood, though I never bumped into Jessie or Nan after our day trip to Portobello.

Earning only £1 a week I was not particularly well off, neither were the McLeods, who experienced the double whammy of a fall in the price of lambs at the same time as the Duke of Cavers increased rents for his farming tenants. We got by, but our big fear was unexpected medical expenses. Doctors were not cheap and when we became ill we relied on home-spun remedies. If we had a chesty cough Mrs McLeod applied an onion and brown bread poultice to our chest at bed time. We often got nits or lice. Conventional wisdom, whether effective or not, was to pour stinging iodine on one's scalp before settling down for the night. The most common ailment was tooth decay, which all too often manifested itself as very painful toothache. If this struck we applied oil of cloves or a drop of whisky to the offending tooth or heated salt put in a sock between one's gum and cheek.. Like the use of poultices these remedies were rarely effective though sometimes provided apparent psychosomatic relief. After the third day of excruciating pain I realised that I would have to see a dentist. But with an extraction costing 5/-, a quarter of my weekly wage, I didn't know what to do. Mr Pringle, one of the five butchers in the High Street, also pulled teeth but rumour had it that was a far from a pleasant experience, often causing even more prolonged pain and discomfort. Hawick did have a visiting dentist who came down from Edinburgh once a week, every Tuesday, and set up a surgery in a room he rented in the Temperance Hotel, known locally as Coffin End, in North Bridge Street.

I had been suffering since Friday afternoon. I missed church on Sunday and on Monday Mr McLeod said he would give me an advance so I could go to the dentist. On Tuesday morning full of fear and trepidation I set off for the town. I was minded by Robbie Burns' description of toothache as 'the hell o' a' diseases'. In the middle of the dental surgeon's temporary surgery was a fearsome looking green and grey chair which the dentist could raise and lower with his foot.

'Do you want gas or are you going to be brave? Gas will cost you an extra 2/6d.'.

I took the coward's way out. I lowered myself into the chair and the dentist sought to attach a tube with a mask at the end to the gas cylinder. He struggled for about five minutes and said, 'I am sorry to say that there is a rip in the tube. I will have to use chloroform. I won't charge you for that'. At least that was a piece of good news. Before I knew it he fetched down a green bottle full of liquid and put some of it on a small hand towel which he placed over my nose and face. I went out like a light and the next thing I knew was that I woke up with a mouthful of blood and a strange but slightly less painful gap at the back of my upper jaw. The dentist said, 'go though to the tea room, don't drink anything but have a wee rest'. After giving him 5/- he gave me a piece of bandage about three feet long and told me to put it round my chin and tie it on the top of my head. 'That's to keep the cold air out of your mouth. Keep it shut, as cold air is not good for the cavity I have created in your gum'. While I was sitting in the tea room I read an old copy of the *Hawick Express* or maybe it was the *Hawick News*. The front page of both papers were full of small classified advertisements. In the middle of the page I noticed a headline which read, *Extracted teeth wanted.* The advert had been placed by a company in Suffolk that bought extracted teeth to make into dentures. They claimed that dentures made with real teeth were far superior to dentures normally made with make-shift wooden teeth. I popped back into the surgery and got the dentist to take my tooth out of the bin. He also gave me three teeth he had extracted earlier in the day. When I sold all of the teeth to the English denture manufactory my visit to Coffin End cost me virtually nothing.

Chapter 4   Shona

1921 - Hawick & Liddesdale

It was three weeks after the King's birthday. I was late and yet I was extremely happy. The King's birthday was never taken too seriously in these parts because of its proximity to the much more important Common Riding. Wee boys still lit celebration bonfires around the town and the high heid yins of the burgh downed a dram and raised their glasses in the loyal toast in the Town Hall. This year the King's Birthday was a special one. That was the day when Gerald had asked my father for my hand in marriage and the day when permission had been granted. We were more ecstatic and in love than ever and found our way down to our secret spot at the burn. We forgot ourselves.

Preparations for the big day dominated our lives and for the first time ever we did not go and watch the Cogsmill ride out. Instead Mum purloined our aged Welsh section D cob and headed off to Bonchester Bridge, the last village before the English border at the Carter Bar. Bonchester had become an enclave for recent immigrants from Italy. A group of families, amongst them the Carluccis and Ceccarellis from the villages of Barga and Picinisco in the province of Lucca in Tuscany had walked to Scotland under the leadership of their padrone to sell their china and porcelain figurines. Their ornaments and the immigrants' pleasant disposition ensured they were welcome as newcomers, although some members of the Free Church were antagonistic because the new arrivals were Roman Catholics. Many of the families decided to stay in the Scottish Borders setting up ice cream parlours and illegal betting shops which they ran from their ice cream carts. Other Italian families became pedlars travelling round the country with a horse and carriage selling various household wares, pots and pans as well as a range of fabrics, thread and ribbons for making clothes. This form of retailing was invaluable for rural dwellers who did not have easy access to high street ironmongers and haberdashers.

Mum was lucky to find Antonio Carlucci at home. During the Common Riding Antonio quickly discovered that most of his customers would be out following the ride outs and not be available to view the sale goods he carried about in his horse and waggon. When Mum told Antonio about the wedding he said, 'this is wonderful news', and told her that he and his wife, Gina, had just given birth to a baby boy, Pietro or Peter. '*Stupendo*. You are going to be a *Nona*'. Little did he realise how true this was.

By coming to his home Mum was able to examine all Antonio's stock in his shed and not the more limited selection she would be shown from the travelling display in the waggon. After much dithering she chose a bolt of pearl-coloured satin for my dress and three yards of richly embroidered Venetian lace for my headdress. She bought some pale blue and green tweed to make a skirt for her mother-of-the-bride outfit.

In the mill all the girls, even Jessie and Nan, were delighted at my news. During the next few weeks phalic-shaped bits of metal from the knitting machines would be left in my handbag and coat pockets. For mill girls in Hawick getting married was something to be celebrated. Each mill had its own traditions and rituals for brides-to-be. While I was looking forward to my ritual humiliation I was also somewhat apprehensive. On the appointed day the girls in my section took hold of my arms and legs and removed my overalls, leaving me only in my slip. They then fastened two Paisley-patterned aprons with a bib to my front and back to conceal my modesty before lifting me into an industrial trolley which was used to ferry bales of wool around the factory. Once sitting down with my knees tucked under my chin in a foetal position they dusted my hair with baby's talcum powder. A large copper pan was then placed over my head so I could not see. To cheers from all the girls I was pushed along between the rows of knitting frames and down the Liddesdale Road to the English Episcopal Church. Every few yards I could feel hands coming over the netting at the sides of the trolley and dropping a range of domestic gifts onto the bottom of the trolley. There was a sieve, a rolling pin, a tattie peeler, an oven glove, a scrubbing brush and lots more like that.

The big day eventually arrived and I was pleased to see that for all but the most eagle-eyed I did not show. Our wedding took place at home where I was christened. Mum had worked for weeks in the dining room which we only used on special occasions making my dress. Shortbread, boxes of fruit along with a wedding cake, other food, bottles of beer, wine and a large flagon of whisky arrived the day before. The guests assembled in the dining room at three o'clock. Dad had invited all the local farming families and a mixture of relatives and other friends. Sadly, and understandably, none of Gerald's family were present although he had had one card and letter of good wishes from his sister. My father was sitting in the big armchair between the window and the fire. People came in in groups, the men with their wives, going over to shake my father's hand before finding somewhere to perch round the room; a couple of the young children were even sitting on the table eyeing the cakes temptingly on display. Gerald was standing nervously next to my father trying not to look too self conscious in a suit, slightly too large for him, he had borrowed from a friend at the angling club. The Rev McAlister entered after all the other guests had arrived. He supped from a glass of red wine; Mum, wearing her new tweed skirt and matching jacket, and I entered last of all; the minister, standing on the hearth rug, turned to Dad and said, 'let us begin'.

We sang the hundredth psalm and Uncle Seth's off-key baritone dominated the room. When asked who giveth this woman away my father raised his hand and waved his shepherd's crook in the air. Gerald and I pledged our troth and promised to love, honour and, in my case, obey. The minister gave us his blessing and we were married. We kissed. There were a couple of coarse comments from the back of the room and we all fell into eating and drinking. It was a bit of a scrum and some of the younger guests went for a walk in the garden. The older farmers went for a snoop round the steading and the women came up to look at my dress and admire my Venetian veil. Tam from over in Teviotdale had brought his fiddle and some of us got up to dance, watched by the wrinkled, whiskered faces of the older shepherds and farmers. Tam's fiddle competed with occasional roars of laughter, the clink and clatter of dishes all combining to emphasise the warmth and inclusivity of humanity. At around half past ten the Rev McAlister said, 'it is time now'. Gerald steered me towards the stairs, lifted me in his arms and to a round of applause, whoops and whistles from the assembled guests took me up to my bedroom. Some of my mill girlfriends had been up earlier transforming the room into a bridal suite. There was white netting hanging from the ceiling, two candles next to the bed and rose petals scattered over the counter pane. This was our private time.

Our wedding took place in August and the months flew by until the time of the birth and my confinement. As a married woman I was expected to give up work and look after my husband. Before we were married we had two wages and even then we found living tough. Mum and Dad helped out and we lived rent-free in one of the farm cottages. Even so times were tight and having a baby was not cheap. Not only did we have to get clothes and other bits and bobs we had to either pay a doctor, a qualified midwife or Mrs Smith, a local farmer's wife, who helped out with the birthing.

She had lots of experience of delivering lambs, calves and piglets as well as babies. The doctor's fee was out of the question. The midwife would charge at least 15/6d. so that left us in the hands of Mrs Smith. She had delivered most of the babies in the neighbourhood and although she lost a few through still-birth or other complications her record of success was not dissimilar to that of the doctor or midwife. I was able to make and knit most of baby's clothes. Terry towelling nappies were a wee bit pricey but Gerald was able to make a crib and fashion a pram out of a large wooden box and set of wheels he found in the steading. We got by.

On the day after the Hobkirk ba' game my waters broke and Gerald was sent to fetch Mrs Smith. She arrived very promptly. Exceptionally, for a first-born, my baby arrived very quickly and with very little of the excruciating pain and discomfort I was warned about by many of the old wives from neighbouring farms. The baby was a boy weighing a healthy 7 lbs 3 oz. Three weeks into his life he was christened Hughie McLeod Singer by the Rev McAlister.

Chapter 5   Hughie

1927- Hawick & Liddesdale

Hughie was an only child. His only regular human contacts, until he went to school, were his nana, papa, mum and dad. In spite of this isolation he was not shy and was the life and soul of the party when he started school. The Moat Primary School at the top of the Fireman's Brae was a big black stone-built place surrounded by railings. There were two gates; both had the date 1897 carved into the lintel. One gate was for the boys, the other for the girls. The school also had some stables at the back of the playground to allow pupils who had to ride their ponies to school to stable and tether their mounts during the day. Hughie rode to school with a new friend Pietro or Peter as they both were considered to live too far away to walk. The two boys eventually rode as a threesome when Pietro's little sister, Bianca started school the following year. Most of the teachers were spinsters and there was a very strict head teacher who was keen on using the belt, a Mr Ross-Gaul. He had been an army officer during the last war and liked everyone to call him Major Ross-Gaul.

We were taught through learning by rote and the repetition method, with the incentive not to make mistakes with the threat of the belt. Mr or rather Major Ross-Gaul seemed to enjoy corporal punishment and considered it a failure if he could not make a child, even the senior boys, cry. As we got older the sums got harder right up to the highest class in the school, the most terrifying class of all with the Major as the class teacher.

Every day started off with the Lord's Prayer and then half an hour of Bible. Going round the class, starting with the dunce in the front row to the dux in the back row, each child read a verse. If we made a mistake we had to learn the verse at home overnight and recite it from the front of the class the following day. We also learned spelling from a little red and white spelling book. We then had to write twelve words out in a grid:

See	six	by
tree	fix	cry
been	box	try
sweet	fox	sky

And if you got two or more wrong you got the belt. Will Grieve who had a striking head of reddish, orange hair and awful body odour was a hopeless speller and took great pride in keeping a record of the times he got the belt - this might be the reason why he was good at counting. When one of the nice girls or clever boys was bad they were made to sit next to Will for the rest of the day. All the teachers knew how to play the piano and we had to learn all the Common Riding songs as well as those written by Robbie Burns like *Flow Gently Sweet Afton*. There were maps all over the wall showing the extent of the British Empire. Most of the teachers were keen on nature studies. We grew crocus bulbs on the window sills and early in the spring jam jars full of frog spawn were left until they became tadpoles looking like a lot of wriggling exclamation marks. We never knew what happened to them at the end of term and suspected they were flushed down the toilet. We were taught how to recognise trees by their leaves - the difference between oak, rowan and ash. We were always having competitions to see who was the best at each subject. Every Friday we were moved around with the pupils with the highest marks sitting on the back row and those with the lowest marks sitting at the front next to the teacher and the black board. That was not the place to be in the Major's class. He was particularly keen on throwing bits of broken chalk at children to get them to pay attention. He was deadly accurate with children in the front row and less so with those further back. Generally speaking Pietro and I tended to sit in the back row, often occupying the dux' desk. On the whole boys and girls learned all the lessons together with the exception of embroidery and woodwork.

When we got to the age of twelve or thirteen we were transferred to the High School. Lessons changed. Work became harder and often more interesting. We did trigonometry and learned Latin. *Hic, haec, hoc* will be forever imprinted on my brain. The girls did domestic science and hockey and the boys metal work and rugby. In those days we did not play rugby at primary school but games of British Bull Dog in the playground prepared us for playing Hawick's favourite sport.

We played rugby twice a week on Tuesday and Thursday afternoons with fixtures against other schools on Saturday mornings before the big game involving the Greens at Mansfield Park. Our rugby teacher was Adam Beattie who was a regular in the Hawick side and had played for Scotland five times. He was more a hero than school teacher. Pietro and I were both good players and we played at half back often interchanging our roles as scrum half and standoff. I was the team goal kicker and went out to practice in front of the posts on the pitch at Volunteer Park next to the school every lunch time. I frequently got into trouble for being late back into class.

Every Friday evening I dubbined and polished my boots as well as washing the long white laces which were hung up in front of the fire to dry in time to lace the boots before breakfast. The big game at the High School was the fixture against Gala Academy. There was one game in particular that I will never forget. While we won and both Pietro and I scored tries and I did not miss a conversion I received two very serious injuries at the same time. I found myself at the bottom of a ruck and the Gala boys gave me a real shoeing. In those days our boots had six leather studs that had nails fixing them to the sole. The stud leather was not particularly hard and over the season wore down leaving some of the nails exposed. At least one of the nails went through my tongue which immediately swelled up and made breathing difficult. In the same ruck their big loose head prop deliberately stamped on my leg snapping my tibia in the process. The game was stopped and a canvas stretcher on wooden poles rushed on to the pitch. Fortunately the Cottage Hospital was just up the hill on the opposite side of Buccleuch Road and four masters carried me up the hill for emergency treatment.

The Cottage Hospital was a single storey Victorian building which had been opened not all that long ago by the Prince of Wales. At the back there was a long tiled corridor leading to a series of wards, an operating theatre, dispensaries and other facilities for the practice of modern medicine. The nurses and sister completed my preparation including sticking a giant syringe of morphia in my backside. The surgeon came to see me. He held my hand tightly and said, 'you can trust me. I used to play for Edinburgh Academicals'. Why I should trust a city-based rugby player with a scalpel in his hands was beyond me.

A porter came to the door and I was lifted on to a trolley. He wheeled me through the admissions ward and along the corridor into the operating theatre. Next to the window overlooking the rugby pitch from where I had come a group of nurses were busy with sponges and an antiseptic spray. One of the nurses with a very large silver buckle on her belt was preparing plaster of Paris. I initially thought she was making me a bowl of porridge. An assistant surgeon in a long sleeveless white coat placed a mask on my face and said count to . . .

The next thing I knew I woke up in the ward with my leg suspended from a pulley above my bed. Mum was there, as was the rector. A rather chubby nurse said, 'how are you feeling? You have been in the wars. At least you beat Gala Academy and I understand your last conversion was the winning margin'. I was feeling nauseous and with some difficulty I avoided throwing up. I was also very thirsty and mum gave me a glass of water. I gulped it down and was told off by the nurse who said I should only have a teaspoon of warm water ever hour on the hour. I fell back asleep. I didn't remember very much of my first few days but when my convalescence started I was constantly annoyed by a very irritating itch on my leg caused by the plaster of Paris. On the fourth day Mum smuggled in a knitting needle which I could squeeze between the plaster and my leg. It provided some relief. Every day I was a little stronger and it was not too long before the plaster came off and they gave me a pair of crutches to help me walk. In some respects I was lucky to break my leg at the end of the season. I had all summer to get my strength back and restore myself to match fitness.

Come September it was my last year at school and my second year of playing for the 1st XV. I was also looking forward to the special outing that Mr Beattie organised for the more experienced members of the school team. That was usually a train trip to Edinburgh to watch a Scotland international at Murrayfield. In 1938 Mr Beattie was more ambitious than usual when he decided with a couple of other masters to take two groups of six boys on a weekend trip to watch Scotland play England at Twickenham.

We set off on the Friday morning on the train down the west coast line. I had never been across the border before and after passing through Newcastelton and steaming through the Debatable Lands we reached Carlisle. Over the next few hours we passed through strange sounding places like Carnforth, Crewe, Solihull and Gerrard's Cross. At a very crowded Euston Station we descended the escalator, walked through a series of very windy tunnels and got on the Tube to Waterloo Station. There we got on an overground Southern Railways train to Richmond where we went to the Elm Guest House in Teddington Avenue. Pietro and I shared a room. We managed to smuggle a couple of bottles of Watney's Red Barrel into the room. It was a little bit more gassy than we were used to but not too bad.

The following day was very special. Scotland had won their previous two matches against Wales and Ireland so as well as playing for the Calcutta Cup we were playing for the Triple Crown. It was a fine spring afternoon. The stadium was packed and King George VI and Queen Elizabeth were in the Royal Box to witness one of the greatest rugby matches ever played. Scotland scored five tries to one in a thrilling encounter and the match was known thereafter as Wilson Shaw's match. Shaw was Scotland's captain and stand off, my position. The final score was Scotland 21, England 16. When the final whistle went we all ran on to the pitch to acclaim our heroes. [*Editor's note: one of the boys from Hawick High School in the other group was the wing forward, one Bill McLaren. Bill went on to become the famous rugby commentator known as the Voice of Rugby. Bill never knew*

that game with the auld enemy was the first rugby match
ever to be televised live. In 1938 very few people had television
sets and with low-powered transmission signals only a few
hundred people living near Twickenham would have seen the
broadcast.].

Pietro and I were both interested in politics and on
Sunday morning we took an early train into Waterloo.
We walked over Hungerford Bridge to Trafalgar
Square, then headed north on to the Mall where we
could see Buckingham Palace in the distance. We crossed
Horseguards Parade and entered Downing Street by the
Park entrance. We stopped outside Number Ten and got
out the Box Brownie to take a souvenir picture at the seat
of power. We then walked down to Parliament Square to
see the Palace of Westminster before getting the Tube
back to Euston to meet up with the rest of our party and
the joyous trip home.

Our political awareness had been heightened ever
since the abdication crisis two years earlier. We were
both worried about Hitler's rise to power and the cruelty
to the Jews on *Kristallnacht*. One of our neighbours,
Bunty Brown, had gone off to fight against fascism in the
Spanish Civil war. There were also very strong rumours
that a small number of homosexual members of our local
Conservative Association went on spying missions to
Germany to provide information to our security services.
Apparently they regularly went on trips to Berlin to
spend time in nightclubs where men were allowed to
dance together - a practice that would result in a jail
sentence in Great Britain. Rumour had it that these clubs
were frequented by the Nazi hierarchy and after a few

schnapps they could be rather indiscreet. Was there any truth in these rumours? Teviotdale and the communities bordering the Hawick to Newcastleton road were prone to gossip so there was likely to be some veracity in the activities of some local queer Tories.

Pietro and I were acutely aware of the rise of fascism in Germany and Italy, given the paternity of both our fathers. Where did that leave us? We would find out.

Chapter 6   Hughie

1939 - Wales & Moncton NB

On September 3rd 1939 I was sitting in the kitchen with Mum and Dad listening to the *Home Service*. The broadcast began, 'This is London. You will now hear a statement from the prime minister'. Mr Chamberlain began, 'I am speaking to you from the Cabinet room in Downing Street. This morning the British Ambassador in Berlin handed the German government a final note saying that if we had not heard from them by 11 o'clock that they were prepared to remove their troops from Poland a state of war would exist between us. I have to tell you now that no such undertaking has been received and consequently this country is at war with Germany'.

'Oh no. Not again.' Mum began to cry.

Following the prime minister's speech there was a series of announcements. All places of entertainment were to close with immediate effect, and people were discouraged from crowding together, unless it was to attend church. About ten minutes later we could hear an unfamiliar wailing on the breeze. Apparently the air raid sirens went off in town accidentally. To all intents and purposes life went on as normal. We had the sheep to look after and all the routine farm jobs to do, but change was in the air. Food became scarcer and all the young men became patriots wanting to join up. Following the earlier war we knew that it would not be long before conscription was enforced. I was coming up to eighteen and Dad was not yet 40. We were both of an age to be called up.

It didn't occur to me that we might both be considered enemy aliens. By the end of September the Aliens Department of the Home Office had set up internment tribunals throughout the country, headed by government officials and local representatives, to examine every UK-registered enemy alien over the age of 16. We were summoned to a tribunal in Galashiels and fortunately, because dad had naturalised in the 1920s, he was considered to be a British citizen. We were classified as category C and to be exempt from both internment and restrictions. Additionally, because my dad was a farmer, he was told that he would be in a reserved occupation and was not likely to be asked to join up. I thought I would have to join the forces. My preference was to be a pilot and shortly after Christmas I was sent to RAF Leuchers in Fife.

The Carluccis were not so fortunate. They had a visit from the police. The Inspector said there was no doubt that Antonio and his wife, Bella, were enemy aliens. He was not so sure about Pietro and Bianca, who had both been born in Bonchester Bridge. The whole family were dispatched to the tribunal in Gala. The Sheriff decreed that the parents were to be interned at Stobs Camp which, after life as a PoW camp and a military training establishment, was converted into an enemy aliens' internment camp, where the men and women lived in separate huts. Because their children had been born in Scotland they were given the choice of going into the camp with their parents or becoming part of the British military. A number of the Carluccis' friends' families had also been faced with this horrendous choice. Pietro knew another second generation Italian immigrant. His acquaintance chose to become a British soldier and joined the KOSBs. Because he took this step his father, mother and grandparents disowned him and threw him out of the family. Sadly when he became a squaddie he was rejected by his so-called comrades and called a garlic-breath Wop or Eyetie. You could not win, so Pietro and Bianca decided to go to Stobs with their parents. After all the camp was only a few miles from where they were born and they already knew some of the locals who helped run the camp.

Nonetheless camp life was harsh. The guards, when they were not seen by their officers would whack the back of the mens legs with their truncheons and the women's and girls' breasts and genitals were a target for guards' hands. Sometimes the women would bribe the guards, offering more than a fumble, for a second ration of food. The camp quickly became overcrowded filling up with Germans and more Italians. The Germans who settled in Scotland tended to be members of the intelligentsia or German Jews escaping from Nazi persecution. They put on plays, sang in a choir and if they had kept their musical instruments it was rumoured that they could have formed a full symphony orchestra. In spite of these distractions life was not pleasant and overcrowding was as big a problem for the authorities as it was for the inmates.

One of the solutions was to ship the aliens off to a third country. Canada, the largest country in the British

Empire, became the destination of choice. This led the Home Office to commission ships. Tragically, on 2 July 1940, the SS Arandora Star, was torpedoed and sunk in the Atlantic en route to Canada. On board were 734 Italians, 438 Germans (including both Nazi sympathisers and Jewish refugees), and 374 British seamen and soldiers. Over half lost their lives, including 470 Italians.

This news did not filter back to Stobs so the Carluccis decided to go to Canada aboard the SS Sobieski, which was escorted by half a dozen frigates - the Sobieski was secretly transporting gold bullion. The Carluccis arrived safely, disembarking at Halifax in Nova Scotia before getting on a train for their onward journey. The sinking of the Arandora Star swayed public opinion in favour of the aliens, many of whom had lived in Britain for a long time before the war. Others had been genuine refugees. The Home Office published a white paper, *Civilian Internees of Enemy Nationality*. The Paper identified categories of persons who could be eligible for release and by the end of 1940 some 10,000 so-called enemy aliens had been freed. This change of policy came too late for the Carluccis who were eventually confined to an internment camp near Fredericton in New Brunswick. There they had a more relaxed time than they would have had at Stobs. While they were allowed to wander about the town they were still locked up and they had to perform labouring tasks such as logging, making mail bags and parachutes.

* * *

Meanwhile, back in Great Britain, I was doing well in my training to fly. I was presented with my wings at the beginning of the summer and promoted to sergeant. The Battle of Britain was underway and, against tremendous odds, the RAF was beginning to get on top of the Luftwaffe. Life expectancy for pilots was just four weeks and there was a constant flow of newly trained pilots being sent to airfields all over the south of England. I had been a bit of a star pupil and I thought I would go straight on to Spitfires. I was mistaken.

One day the squadron leader called me into his office. 'Sergeant Singer, you have impressed your teachers and have all the makings of becoming an outstanding flier. We need people like you. With an ever increasing demand for new pilots the wing commander has asked me to send our best new pilots on a special fast-track course at Fairwood Common in Swansea to become flying instructors. There you will learn everything you need to know and gain experience of flying Tiger Moths, Link Trainers, Ansons, Oxfords, A T 10s and others'.

Discipline was strict and the demands placed on trainee instructors were exceptionally high. In a very short time I had to confirm, with my signature, that I understood the petrol systems, hydraulic brakes (including the emergency system) and actions to be taken in the event of a fire for every aircraft I flew or taught in. All this and more had to be performed to set standards. One of the first entries in my log book read; 'I certify that I, Hughie McLeod Singer, have been instructed in air screw swinging in accordance with standard procedure as laid down in A.P. 129 (F.T.M. part 1 chap 11 para 24) and Supplement of Reserve's Instruction No, 9 Section.2'.

It was a hard slog. We were accommodated in long wooden huts, which had a striking resemblance to the huts at Stobs camp. The huts were of a wooden construction and built to accommodate 20 personnel in small rooms, each containing a cupboard, a bed, some shelves and a desk for studying; a bare bulb hung from the ceiling. There was a common room at one end filled with a motley collection of second-hand Artdeco furniture and a wash room at the rear. The huts at Stobs were of a similar size. At Stobs there was no room to socialise and each hut accommodated 60 inmates in bunk beds. There was only one latrine for which there was always a long queue to enter its malodorous depths. Social life was good at Fairwood Common. Welsh beer wasn't bad. It was a lot less gassy than that I experienced in London. Naturally, being located in West Wales, there was a rugby team. The base had a fairly good side and I got the opportunity to play outside Bledwynn Williams, the Pontypool scrum half who had been on the fringes of the Welsh side before war broke out.

We were at Fairwood Common to learn. Work was hard. Most of our time was spent in the classroom, the cockpit, the hangers or studying in our pokey bedrooms. At our first classroom session we were given a 36 point list of processes and procedures we had to instruct trainee pilots in. We were targeted to become fully familiar with the training programme which was designed to teach young men to become competent enough to attempt their first solo flight. All this learning had to be completed and fully understood in the first four weeks of training. The syllabus included:

1. Introduction to aircraft and air experience
2. Effect of controls
3. Straight and level flight
4. Climbing and descending
5. Taxying
6. Medium level turns
7. Further effect of controls
8. Stalling
9. Climbing and gliding turns
10. Take-off into wind
11. Circuits
12. Approach and landing into wind
13. Going round again
14. Spinning
15. Solo flying
16. I/F the instruments
17. Nav: course flying
18. Nav: turning on to course
19. Nav: map reading and pinpointing
20. Sideslipping
21. I/F straight and level flying
22. Stoop turns
23. I/F climbing and descending
24. Low-flying
25. I/F climbing and descending turns
26. Precautionary landings

27. Forced landings
28. I/F taking off
29. Taking off out of wind
30. Circuits
31. Landing out of wind
32. Emergency; fire, abandoning, restarting engine
33. I/F spinning
34. Aerobatics
35. Night flying
36. Overshoot procedure.

We were taught how to grade students into below average, average or above average. We were advised some students could be graded as exceptional as had all my comrades in this advanced training school. Students who passed muster were to be given a proficiency assessment signed by the Station Commander and those below average eliminated for further training or flying duties.

Given the shortage of aircraft and the limited experience and short time students and their instructors spent in the air, accidents were inevitable. There was a very rigorous safety regime and the requirement to keep detailed records whenever anything went awry. When someone had caused an accident or who had been involved in an accident what happened had to be recorded in personal log books. This information and any further investigation deemed necessary would be used to determine whether the accident had been caused by an error of judgement, carelessness, gross carelessness or mechanical failure. Regulations stipulated that in cases of gross carelessness red ink should be used and that this entry should be made opposite the details of the flight on which the accident occurred. Flying gave us a wonderful feeling of freedom, being at one with the skies and clouds but behind it all was hard graft involving a boring, bureaucratic attention to detail and record keeping that was insisted upon by the civil servants at the Ministry of Defence. I spent four months in Wales. At the end of my time I was called into the station commander's office. He said that I had passed out as above average and that I was ready to be given my first posting.

In the early years of the war the Luftwaffe bombed areas throughout Great Britain. Places like London, Coventry and Glasgow were relentlessly targeted but even places like Swansea, where I was based was occasionally bombed - even Hawick suffered casualties when the Jerrys dropped a group of incendiaries on the tank depot in Weensland Road. Being selfish, I was pleased that new pilots were trained in areas safe from enemy bombing. I was offered three locations: Potchefstroom in South Africa, Turner Field in the USA or Moncton in Canada. I don't know why, but I chose Canada.

I was given ten days leave, three of which were spent travelling home and another two travelling to Liverpool to embark on the SS Mauritania, which had been converted into a troop ship. I was aware of the risks of being sunk by U-boats, but was told by the Purser that the German Navy had been concentrating their efforts on shipping travelling in the opposite direction bringing much needed supplies to war-torn Britain. Even so we were accompanied by a frigate and for the first few hundred miles out into the North Atlantic we could see and hear Sunderland and Swordfish aircraft offering us protective cover. Even so the captain of the Mauritania travelled in a zig zag pattern across the ocean. This made for an uncomfortable passage as we were obliged to go broadside against high stormy waves. After 14 days we arrived at Pier 21 in Halifax, Nova Scotia.

It was the middle of September. The war had been going on for three years. The weather was a balmy 70° F. We were told that in six to eight weeks it would fall to 28° F below zero. Brrrr. I wasn't looking forward to that. We were used to cold winters at Rubers Hill but nothing quite like that. I couldn't believe it when we were told that if it fell to -40° F we had to keep our mouths shut because our fillings could contract and fall out of our mouths. But when we arrived it was warm and we soon found that insect life was different in New Brunswick. We were plagued by black fly and their bite was fearsome, making our midges and clegs appear almost benign. We were all struck by the volume and density of the trees. When we were up in the air the green canopy below swayed like the waves in a green ocean. You could see where settlements had been hued out of the arboreal ground cover. The airfield stood out, surrounded by acre upon acre of undulating and oscillating corn. I had never had sweetcorn before and enjoyed it roasted on the fire pit outside the mess. This way of life did not take long to get used to but what was strange, and a very pleasant change from rationing back home, was the choice and abundance of food. The Canadians had salads with everything. A sandwich was invariably accompanied with French fries. I ate vegetables, like broccoli, I had never had before and we all found it strange to eat rice as part of a main course and not as a pudding.

As well as six other flying instructors the Mauritania shipped over trainee pilots from England, Scotland and Wales as well as a cohort of very exuberant Poles. They were to join 40 or so Canadian trainee pilots from the RCAF. Training regimes were rigorous and after doing the same drills over and over with different aspiring pilots it soon became monotonous. In my log book I recorded an average of 16.45 hours of instructional flying time a month, 178.00 hours of instructional time and 4 hours 10 minutes of other flying. We were obliged to keep very detailed records in our log books. These entries would be signed by myself and checked by the squadron leader. The last typed instruction on the inside front cover was threatening: 'Pilot's Log Books are official documents and any untidiness or lack of attention to detail will receive appropriate disciplinary action'. I came to appreciate the value of the time I had spent under the threat of Major Ross-Gaul's ruler rapping my knuckles if my joined up writing strayed off the line.

Much of my time was devoted to planning activities, tasks and targets for the trainees. My first four trainees were AC2C Abraham, AC2C Cowley, P/P Dunanowski and P/P Walker. A typical weekly programme would involve:

Exercises

1 (a) Familiarisation and orientation
   (b) Instrument flying refresher
2 Figures of eight at a constant height
3 Complete approach

Hooded

4 Figures of eight at constant height
5 (a) Complete approach
   (b) Back beam approach
6 (a) Approaches with visual indicator only
   (b) Approaches with beam signals only
7 Homing with Q.O.M.
8 Timing without Q.O.M.
9 Cross country

Carrying out these routines day after day, sometimes after scraping ice off the wings and fuselage, and other times spent in an indoor classroom grounded by the weather, was extremely monotonous. Free time was scarce but I did learn to ice skate and I was the skip of our curling team. At home we had a rink nearby between Williestruther and Flex.

There were few signs that the war was going to come to an end soon. Our forces were bogged down in North Africa and the Hun was floundering inconclusively on the Russian Steppes. What kept me going were the regular letters I had from Mum and Dad. Towards the end of the war the Canadian Government and Canada

Post created armed forces aerogrammes. These were printed on light-weight grey paper with folds that had to be glued together. On the face was printed, 'Forces Air Letter/Lettre-avion pour militaire'. While on the back, 'No enclosures permitted/Ne rien insérer' and 'Authorized by the Canada Post Corporation for mailing in Canada/Autorisé par la Société Canadienne des Postes pour mise à la poste au Canada'.These new aerogrammes proved so popular that the Royal Mail in the UK introduced a blue version for families at home to communicate with their loved ones fighting overseas.

There was only a limited amount of space on these air letter forms so one could only write fairly short newsy letters. Once, to wish me happy birthday, Mum went over the top. She had so much to say about what was going on at the farm as well as about the sad loss of Ian Gowrie, the son of the local pig farmer who was killed in action in Tangiers, that her writing was so small that I almost needed a magnifying glass to read it. Once I had described my life in Canada there was little else to write about. I was also conscious the censor would not like me to provide any information that might be considered to benefit the enemy, so my letters almost became as repetitive as my life on the station. After a year or so in Moncton I was able to write about my plans for the leave that was due to me. The daily routine, while full of adrenaline and excitement for the trainee pilots, for me was more of the same, humdrum and mind-numbing. Two weeks of leave were something to look forward to, to plan, anticipate and write home about. Obviously I could not return home but the attractions in New Brunswick and the immediate environs were appealing. Nearby were the Gulf of St Lawrence, Prince Edward Island, Nova Scotia, and Cape Breton and to the south the State of Maine in the USA. The problem was that travel was not all that easy in war time and it was more expensive than my limited wages could really afford. Even so there was so much to see and even if I had to restrict myself to staying in New Brunswick which was about the size of Scotland there were lots of new things to see and experience. Eastern Canada Greyhound Lines provided a fairly comprehensive, regular and cheap bus service throughout the Province so I plumped to travel to St John and Fredericton. My days, when I was not flying, were filled with a sense of anticipation and excitement. St John sounded a really interesting place to visit - being the oldest city in Canada. From my reading I learned it was originally inhabited by the Mi'kmaq and Wolastoqiyik tribes before being fought over by the French and the British. During the American Civil war thousands of refugees who wished to remain British arrived from the south. To me the most striking thing about St John was its position on the Bay of Fundy where it was joined by the St John River creating a most peculiar reverse tidal surge called the Reversing Falls. I told Mum all about that and the old forts I would visit and the restaurants where I would eat lobster, an unheard of delicacy in the rural Scottish Borders. From St John I planned to travel to Fredericton, the provincial capital. It was also home to thousands of people of Scottish ancestry.

It seemed an age before the time for my leave arrived, then early one Saturday morning, I made my way to the Maritime Bus Station downtown and stood in line on the stance for the Greyhound bus to St John and further afield.

Chapter 7   Bianca

1940 - Bonchester Bridge & Fredericton NB

The Carlucci family, shortly after they decided to leave Stobs to go to Canada, were escorted by guards to the railway station to start their journey to Liverpool, their port of embarkation. Their departure was a much quieter affair than when they were taken from their home in Bonchester Bridge to go to Stobs camp. On that occasion most residents came out of their front doors along with lunch-time drinkers in the Fox and Hounds to see them off. Their reception was mixed. There were some jeers calling them to fuck off while other people, who had come to look on this Italian family as their friends, cried, 'shame' and 'you'll be welcome back when Adolf and Mussolini are defeated'.

At Hawick Station they were locked in the guard's van and after what seemed like days with only stale bread and water were eventually decanted onto the platform at Lime Street in Liverpool. The men and women were separated and hustled on to a bus that took them to the docks. In a large shed they were stripped, given a hunk of pink Lifebuoy soap, hosed down with cold water and told to dry themselves in double quick time. The two suitcases holding their personal possessions were confiscated, never to be seen again. The next fifteen days of a very rough crossing when they never saw daylight are best forgotten.

The family were summarily deposited in the hold and stacked in bunks one on top of another on top of another. The stench of vomit and other human waste was unbearable.

After arrival on Partridge Island in the Bay of Fundy the Carluccis were sprayed with DDT and helped up on to military transport trucks with canvas roofs and cold metal benches to sit on. Eight bumpy hours later, with one stop for watery gruel and stale bread, they arrived at the Fredericton internment camp. It had a feel of Stobs about it. The Canadian huts were about the same size, though they were painted white with much steeper roofs to ensure the snow slid off and would not weigh down the purlins. Antonio, as head of the family, had tried throughout the nightmare of recent days to maintain positivity and family morale with a stream of jokes and anecdotes. On arrival at the camp he observed, 'look at the doors. They open inwards. The idiots who designed Stobs Camp had doors that opened outwards. After one winter storm the inmates couldn't open the door because of the weight of snow. The guards had to dig them out'.

There were only a handful of enemy aliens from Britain in the Fredericton Camp. The majority were formerly Canadian residents who were forcibly detained under the War Measures Act. The majority hailed from combatant countries such as Germany, Japan, and Italy and most, unlike the Carluccis, were fascist sympathisers. Camp life was tough but the Carluccis enjoyed speaking Italian with other people on a regular basis. Conditions were trying. The guards were sometimes brutal. Resentment at what many regarded as their unjust confinement was widespread. This provoked resistance — some passive, such as work slowdowns. Other efforts were more determined. There were some escape attempts but not one inmate ever seemed to get away. The whole family was put to work logging in the surrounding forests at a measly 50c per day. The money was worth next to nothing, especially as there was nothing to spend it on in the camp. Amongst inmates the main currency was cigarettes and as none of the Carlucci family smoked they decided to keep their money in a hollowed-out post in Antonio's bunk and save it to spend on the one day a quarter the inmates were allowed to visit the nearby city of Fredericton.

Bianca was a pretty girl and she attracted the attention of many of the male prisoners. She got on especially well with a handsome young man called Claudio Houde. Claudio was the brother of Camillien Houde. Claudio had been separated from his more famous sibling when they were both imprisoned in Ontario. Camillien, the elder of the two brothers, was the popular mayor of Montreal. Houde was a fascist sympathiser. After calling for defiance of registration for military service Houde was arrested at city hall by the RCMP and interned in Ontario. Like many nationalist French Canadians of the period, he supported the ideology of Mussolini's Italy and Vichy France.

Like Bianca, her family and most other inmates, Claudio was also on logging duties. Fredericton was surrounded by old-growth forests. These woodlands were dark, magical and occasionally threatening places with towering, mossy Sitka spruce trees and gnarly red cedars with trunks wider than a car's length. There were Garry oak and arbutus trees, massive Douglas firs as well as slow-growing yellow cedars and mountain hemlocks covered in beard lichens. It was a near pre-historic environment. The woodland, which had been there for a very long time, also provided the perfect habitat for endangered wildlife such as the spotted owl and marbled murrelet. More common were black bears, chipmunks, racoons, skunks, giant elks and the occasional wild cat. Old logging hands, who had been interned for longer than us, gave us contradictory advice about what to do in the event of a rare bear encounter. There were some that said that bears never come near us because we would be making too much noise. Others said that was baloney and that if we didn't keep our lunch-time snap wrapped up to prevent bears smelling it or if we accidentally came across a bear cub we had to take immediate action. Again we got contradictory advice. Some said run, others said stand still, not engage eye contact and to raise your arms to make yourself look as big as possible then slowly back away. Others said lie down and play dead. We never encountered a bear but we did appreciate the advice about never to touch or get near a skunk - the smell was disgusting, long lasting and difficult to get rid of.

Every weekday morning at half past seven we poured out of our warm steamy huts - strangely, that clammy environment remained unchanged throughout the year - to stand in three lines to answer our names during roll call. With that over the guard yelled,

'Attenshun. To your left in threes. Quick march'. We then piled into large trucks, the same ones that brought us to the camp. The journey to the area of forest where we were working sometimes only took a quarter of an hour. Sometimes it was as long as an hour and a half.

The forests round Fredericton were dotted with lakes which fed tributaries to the St John River. Spread around lake edges as well as in the hinterland of the woodland was cottage country. Many city dwellers in the pursuit of the outdoors built timber-frame cottages or hunting lodges. These vacation and weekend dwellings typically had two or three bedrooms, a large living kitchen with a range and wood-burner. Out front was a porch with an Adirondack or rocking chair. There was, invariably, a fire pit or built-in barbecue. Underneath the cottage was a basement or crawl space. Outside there was sometimes an ice house and if the house had a lake frontage there was often a wooden dock with a canoe tied up alongside.

There was a scattering of cottages round Killarney Lake where I had been working with the logging squad. We even came across an isolated cottage in the depths of the forest in a clearing at the end of of one of the many meandering trails and animal tracks. It was in this cottage where I would encounter a life-changing experience.

I was not unfamiliar with logging work, though I had never done any myself. After the First World War the British government created the Forestry Commission to restore the nation's woodland after war-time depletion. Wauchope Forest was created near my home in Bonchester Bridge. Vast though it was to us at the time, it was very small scale compared with Canadian forests. It was also very different from the old growth in one other respect. It was largely a single species forest. There were rows and rows of monotonous Sitka Spruce interrupted every now and then by a firebreak.

Another difference was that the Forestry Commission only employed men - forestry was not considered women's work. In New Brunswick there was some allowance made for the weaker sex. We were saved from the strenuous work of felling trees and hitching them up to a horse or tractor to be dragged off to the river where 30 or so of the bare trunks were tied together in cribs and were then floated down the river to a timber mill, downstream. The women's job was to feed the branches into an industrial chipper. The chips we produced were used as a fuel and for paper-making. The chipper we used was an old German Jensen machine. It was always breaking down which was good because we could take a break and chat with the other girls.

One day during a breakdown this tall, handsome, swarthy man appeared on the edge of our group. We all stopped to have a look. It was a hot day and he had taken off his striped prison shirt. He was sun-tanned and the sweat stood out on his muscular chest. Suddenly there was a loud whistle and the shriek of a guard, 'Houde, what the fuck do you think you are doing? Get back to work'.

'I was only trying to see if I could get this old Jensen chipper working again'.

'Bugger that. Your job is to fell trees'. The muscular lumberjack turned away, not before giving us a sly wink, and went back to work. That was the last time we saw Houde for a number of weeks. One day, on the way back to the camp, he boldly approached and said, 'you are that Scottish girl aren't you?'

For some strange reason I answered in Italian, '*certo*'.

'You have a Scottish accent'.

'And you have a strange mixture of Quebecois patois, and American accents'. I paused, 'how do you know what a Scottish accent sounds like'?

He smiled, and said 'I have a number of Scottish friends, Irish ones and Japanese, even strange Mennonite ones. I am interested in their accents'. He went on, 'Canada is a melting pot of different immigrant nationalities and that, strangely enough is why I am here. I come from Quebec and we resent being ruled by the English. The Canadian government is Anglophile and the centre of power in Ottawa likes to think of itself as, the most important country in the so-called British Empire after England. What they don't realise is that, in reality, Canada is a country of immigrants from places like Germany, Italy, Austria, Ireland and Japan, all countries that despise the English and are currently at war. The bastards have locked me up' and with in a twinkle in his eye added, 'the only good thing is that at least I have met you'.

This was the most intellectual conversation I had had since I was forcibly removed from Hawick High School. I found it stimulating and with his dashing looks not unlike the Hollywood star, Rudolf Valentino, I was all a flutter when we got down from the truck and went off for our evening meal.

Chapter 8 Claudio

1942 - Fredericton NB

Claudio's brother Camillien Houde was a godfather-like figure in the city of Montreal and throughout Quebec. He was a tall man with a protruding Roman nose, slicked-back, black, brilliantined hair and, like Winston Churchill, routinely had a big fat cigar clamped between his lips. He was a political giant who served at city, provincial and federal levels dispensing largesse and favours to people who could keep him in power. Corruption was second nature and he grew rich during the Great Depression turning a blind eye to brothels and sundry city racketeers. Originally from the Loire region of France Houde's ancestors emigrated to New France as long ago as the seventeenth century. The family made their money in banking and biscuit manufacturing. Claudio was considerably younger than his older brother. As the little brother he looked up to Camillien and became his general factotum performing all sorts of unsavoury tasks to maintain his brother's status and position.

As such Claudio ran a secret cadre of heavies - all of whom were committed to Quebecois nationalism. They resented the dominance and superiority of the Anglophiles and the control they effected over Ottawa, Quebec and the rest of Canada. Behind the scenes Claudio ran a subversive anti-Anglophile group that planned violence and sabotage against the Federal authorities. Claudio's most trusted henchman was a Fenian Irishman, Paddy O'Rourke.

The Fenians had a lot in common with Quebecois nationalists. We were both Catholic and we both opposed Protestant English dominance with a passion. Ever since Samuel de Champlain established New France in Eastern Canada at the beginning of the seventeenth century we were always battling the English. Even so, I think that Irish resentment of the English goes back even further. Actually, come to think of it, the French never really got on with the English either, even after William from Normandy landed at Hastings in 1066. I learned from Paddy that his father and grandfather had been involved with the movement that sought to end English rule in Ireland. After the Great Famine in the 1840s tens of thousands of starving Irish families emigrated to America and Canada. Anti-English sentiment among this community was widespread and groups of radicals formed the Fenian Brotherhood in the United States. These Fenians did not have much to gripe about in an independent USA that had thrown out George III. They turned their attention to the North where Queen Victoria, who never visited Canada, was Empress and Queen, And so began a series of Fenian raids and sabotage in Canada. This was Paddy's legacy - he was a good man to have on our side. Paddy especially enjoyed telling us that his great granny had been a distant relative of Patrick Whelan who famously assassinated Thomas D'Arcy McGee, a well known member of the Canadian Parliament, in downtown Ottawa in 1868.

The Fenians were a long established, oath-bound, secretive organisation. My brother Camillien, on my 21st birthday, asked me to find out as much as I could about how they operated as we had a lot to learn from their success. Only a few years before, the Irish Republic had been established in Dublin when the forces of Empire had been roundly defeated. I started on this mission by frequenting Irish bars on the waterfront of the St Lawrence in Montreal. I soon found that Mckibbin's Bar on Bishop street was a Fenian haunt. At first the clientele were suspicious of a Montréaler but after a few weeks of downing black Irish stout and playing cards I gradually became one of the boys. Mckibbin's was dominated by a long walnut bar. There was a pother of pipe and cigarette smoke, the twang of Irish accents and on some nights fiddlers, a penny whistle player and someone on a bodhran. The landlady was the ironically named Mrs England. She was quite a woman, supporting women's suffrage and becoming one of the first women to graduate from McGill University. As a radical feminist campaigner she provided the Fenians with the ideal cover for their activities.

The black stuff was a great tongue loosener and Paddy O'Rourke soon revealed that they had a network of secret cells throughout Quebec, Ontario, New Brunswick and Nova Scotia. Arms and explosives were secretly smuggled on board cargo ships from Ireland and landed at small ports like those in the Gaspé peninsula and Pugwash. Others were smuggled over the long unguarded border with the USA. On the night when I was sworn into the Brotherhood I told Paddy and his comrades that my brother owned a cottage deep in the forest near the appropriately named Lake Killarney in New Brunswick.The location was out of sight, in a lonely part of the forest and ideally situated as a base for supporting action in the provincial capital of Fredericton. My offer of the cottage was warmly welcomed and it was designated a sleeper for a future campaign.

Along with my brother I was arrested in Montreal in 1940 for sedition. Our open support for Mussolini and Vichy France was too much for the authorities. Camillien had expressed his doubts about Canada's support and involvement in the war on several occasions. When Prime Minister Mackenzie King introduced the National Resources Mobilization Act obliging virtually all Canadians 16 and over, male and female alike, to complete detailed registration forms this was a step too far for Camillien. My older brother was staunchly opposed to the idea of conscription and the idea of Canadian forces fighting overseas. He publicly stated this to a group of journalists and in coruscating editorials condemning his views the RCMP stepped in. We were both incarcerated at the Petawawa Internment Camp in Ontario. Shortly after our arrival we were separated and I was moved to the camp at Fredericton.

En route to New Brunswick Claudio tried to work out in his mind why they had been separated. He mused: *I was different from Camillien. He was a larger than life character and a mass of contradictions. In some respects he acted like the Chicago Mafia but in others he was a staunch*

Conservative member of the establishment. He was passionate about independence for Quebec yet he was an admirer of the royal family, having met the king and queen before the war. In comparison I was not so conflicted. I wanted Quebec separatism. I wanted it now. The state, the English, the British Empire were the enemy. Violence and subversion were the best way to achieve our aims.

Meeting the inmates at the Fredericton camp was a revelation for Claudio. In one place he found a concentration of like-minded sympathisers. There were Germans, Italians and other fascist supporters as well as others who hated the English with whom they were at war. In addition there were more than a few Irish immigrants to Canada who the Canadian authorities thought best to lock away for the duration.

By a twist of fate I was billeted in the same hut with my old friend from Montreal, Paddy O'Rourke. He told me he had been arrested for daubing the wall outside the British High Commissioner's residence on Sussex Drive in Ottawa with: "Up the IRA". We hit it off again, two like-minded young men with a pathological hatred of the English. What's more we were prepared to go to any lengths.

Paddy reminded me all about his involvement with the Brotherhood in the States. He explained how they were organised into secret cells throughout the northern states, from New York to Chicago and over the St Lawrence to Ontario and eastern Canada. Secrecy was assured and names were not shared to keep things secure. While theoretically not on active service the cells were in a permanent state of readiness, training and storing arms, explosives and ammunition. What they were intending to do was not clear but there was an underlying desire to inflict damage on the British State and to return the six counties in Northern Ireland to Dublin rule. We both realised that the people of Quebec were caught on the horns of the same dilemma.

One night after lights out I whispered. 'Paddy I am sure I told you that my brother Camillien is rich and powerful and has a cottage in the depths of the forest near Killarney Lake where we are felling trees? It is currently empty and its isolation could make it the perfect place to store guns and explosives'.

He replied, 'can we go and have a look at it'?

'The next time we are in the area and when we can escape the attention of the guards. That should be easy as there are only two of them to thirty of us in the detail working over a very wide area'.

Three weeks later we managed to escape the guards' scrutiny.

Paddy was very excited. 'This is perfect. No one comes near it and it is large enough to billet a squad as well as having a crawl space to conceal weapons and an empty ice house some 50 yards away where we can store explosives. I've got a snitch amongst the guards who will deliver a message to the boys in the cell in Androscoggin in Maine. If you can let me know where a key will be concealed they will start delivering as soon as is practical'.

The cottage remained empty for weeks but having revisited it I thought it would be the perfect place in which to plan assignations with the Scottish girl who had caught my eye. We enjoyed a lovely summer.

Chapter 9   Bianca

1943 - Fredericton NB

Towards the end of June I was hauled off the truck taking the work detail to the forest and marched into the camp office. I was told to sit down, The door was slammed shut and I heard a key turn in the lock. I sat on the hard wooden chair in front of a desk with an overflowing ash tray on it. There were two wooden chairs on the other side of the table. Why on earth was I here? What had I done? I was left on my own for what seemed like hours getting more and more nervous as time wore on.

I heard the key in the lock and in walked two enormous men in black RCMP uniforms. One had sergeant stripes on his arms, the other some form of insignia on his epaulettes. The sergeant's face was grim. The lines on his forehead resembled railway tracks above two very bushy eyebrows and a thick moustache that appeared to spread from ear to ear. The other guy had a much pleasanter appearance. The sergeant, opening a pack of Marlboro said, 'cigarette'?

'No thank you. I don't smoke'.

The officer immediately said, 'I'll come straight to the point. We understand that you have become rather friendly with Claudio Houde and that you disappear off with him to a cottage in the forest. We want you to spy on him'.

'Why? What has he supposed to have done? Why me?' I was taken completely by surprise.

'Look missy', snarled the sergeant. 'We are not messing around. If you don't do what we ask we are going to ship you, your parents and brother off to a very unpleasant secret prison camp in the Northern Territories where your piss will freeze before it hits the ground'.

'I don't think we need go that far,' said the officer. 'Look we have been looking into your background. You were born in Scotland and are a British subject. You should not be imprisoned as an enemy alien. You are one of us. We think that, no, we know that Claudio Houde is a dangerous subversive and we need to know what he is up to. If you help us we can make life very much more bearable for you and your family as well as giving you permission to stay in Canada after the war if you would prefer not to go back to England. And, we will allow you to go into town every Saturday rather than the couple of hours a month you are allowed now'.

I still did not know what to say but nodded.

'The bastard Houde and a coterie of other ne'er-do-wells are preparing to set off a series of explosions in Fredericton. We need to know where, when and how. You have a relationship with this guy I am sure you can wheedle it out of him'.

'How'?

'Come on a bright young lass like you must know.' The sergeant had a lascivious grin on his face. 'You just drop your knickers and part your legs and he will be putty in your hands'.

'I can't do that. I have told Claudio countless times that I am saving myself until I am married, and, I mean it'.

'Well you'll just have to be more subtle and devious', rejoined the officer.

'I haven't said I will be your spy yet'.

'Well you fucking well better agree', said the sergeant. Otherwise your brother and father are destined to freeze their nuts off'.

The officer, obviously playing the good cop said, 'we'll give you half an hour to think about it. In the meantime we'll have a coffee and sandwich brought in for you'. They got up and left.

I was shaking. I didn't know what to do. Claudio was such a lovely man. I couldn't believe he was a subversive terrorist. How could I wheedle information out of him without him suspecting that my attitude towards him had changed? And would I be able to stop fancying him? His hand had never gone above my suspender belt and he must have become used to me pushing him away. I could probably pretend that nothing had changed in our relationship and I could gain his trust to such a degree that he might share his secrets. I had never let on that my true allegiance was towards Scotland, where I had been born and brought up. My Italian ancestry was only an accident of my birth. The fact that I was considered an enemy alien was because, at the tribunal in Galashiels, I chose to remain with my parents who were Italian and we were therefore deemed to be enemy aliens. If I had chosen not to go to Stobs, which was an option, I risked Mum and Dad despising me and disowning me. My family loyalty was stronger than anything else. Keeping all this to myself I probably could trick Claudio into thinking I was on his side. I was still shaking when the Mounties came back into the room. I decided to play along with them and to lighten the atmosphere I asked, 'why aren't you wearing your stetsons and are your horses tied up outside?'

'Very funny', growled the sergeant.

The officer smiled. 'Have you had a chance to think about what we want you to do'?

'Yes'. I hesitated. I didn't want them to think I was a push over.

'Well have you'? said the sergeant in a much more reasonable tone.

'I have. What do you want me to find out and how will I get information to you'?

They told me I had to find out what was stored in the cottage. Were there guns, ammunition and explosives? I was told to look if there was a basement or crawl space and what was in the icehouse. They knew that there were arms in the cottage but not what or how many. Nor did they know how Claudio planned to use them or how the weapons were delivered to the cottage and where they came from. They told me that Claudio would be working with others. Could I find out their names and did any of them stay in the cottage? This briefing went on for over an hour then more sandwiches and coffee were brought in.

'You are doing well lass'. The sergeant was much more favourably disposed towards me now. 'We'll be offering you and your family Canadian citizenship and a pardon if you can carry all this off'.

I spent the rest of the afternoon being taught how to be a spy. I wasn't expected to be a Mata Hari. I was told to keep my eyes and ears open, to check out the rooms and crawl space in the cottage as well as the ice house. They advised me not to be too obvious when asking questions and to carefully remember what I was told. I was advised to be natural but wary, that I could easily give myself away. They warned that if Claudio became suspicious there was little they could do to help.

Over the coming weeks I would bump into Claudio in the truck on the way to work. We could talk quite openly but this never went beyond flirting and occasionally arranging secret assignations in the cottage when our work details were nearby and the guards' attention was elsewhere or when they were having a complacent smoke to relieve their boredom.

On the second of these occasions I was able to get into one of the bedrooms alone when he went off to what he called the John. Inside the bedroom there were six wooden boxes with a series of numbers and the words Lee Enfield stencilled in black. I knew that they were rifles. We had been taught at school that John Lee, who invented the bolt-action rifle, had been born in Hawick before emigrating to Canada. I carefully committed to memory the quantity and dimensions of the boxes. Two days later I left the rather tattered curtains next to my bunk closed. This was the signal to let the Mounties know that I had something to tell them.

On the way back from work the following day the guards started shouting at me and accusing me of slacking and that I wasn't working hard enough. One of them slapped me on the face and told me to report to the Guard Hut before I went to the mess to be fed. Inside the hut, reeking of cigarette smoke, were the two Mounties. I told them what I had found. They were pleased with me and said my whole family could spend Saturday in Fredericton and to avoid suspicion of favouritism all the inhabitants of my hut would be awarded the privilege of a day out in town. I was given $5.00 to spend. I was asked if I had been able to explore the crawl space undetected, mentioning as an afterthought that I should be cautious about checking out the ice house. It was some way from the cottage and it was considered that it could be too risky to go there undetected. Over the coming weeks I did manage to get into the crawl space when Claudio had a bout of diarrhoea and had prolonged spells in the John. The space under the cottage was half full of boxes of bullets and what to me looked like sticks of dynamite. The Mounties were really pleased when I reported this find.

Over time, during my visits to the cottage, I noticed that one of the beds had been slept in. I asked Claudio about this and he said that one of Paddy O'Rourke's friends from across the Border in Maine came across now and again to go fishing in Lake Killarney where the pickerel were reported to be particularly plentiful. I said, 'that's a long way to come to go fishing'.

Claudio looked at me with a curious mixture of doubt and trust in his expression. 'We have known each other for a long time and I think you think the same way as me. You hate the English just like me. Don't you'? I nodded vigorously. 'Well Eamon did not come to fish. He belongs to the same group of patriots as me and Paddy. Over recent months he has been smuggling weapons over the border at Trump Falls for use in some action we have planned in these parts. He and a couple of comrades come over when there is a full moon so he can find his way through the dense forest in the dark. They only stayed the night because when leaving to go back to the States they found a couple of bears sniffing around in the yard and thought it better to postpone their departure. They did not want to shoot them and attract attention.

This was just the news the Mounties wanted to hear. An ambush was set up on the Canadian side of the Border at the next full moon and three Fenian smugglers were arrested and one was killed during a brief exchange of fire. When this was going on Claudio was arrested, removed from his hut, and eventually sent to Kingston Maximum Security Penitentiary. I never saw him again.

Chapter 10   Hughie

1944 - Moncton & Fredericton NB

The time for my leave eventually came round. I had not had a prolonged break since before I was posted to Swansea. I was ready for a bit of what the Canadians called R&R.

After a fascinating time exploring the Bay of Fundy and its extraordinary tides I headed off to Fredericton. I had arranged bed and breakfast accommodation at Champlain House about ten minutes walk from the river and near Wilmot Park. The B&B was an imposing two-storey, red timber building with steep roofs covered in wooden shingles. There was a patio on two sides of the house fringed with intricate blue and white tracery that gave the property a strangely Victorian appearance. There were four guest bedrooms on the first floor with a bathroom at the end of the corridor. Being early in the season I had the place to myself. The landlady was Dutch, a Mrs De Kuyper. She was a jolly, robust lady who had emigrated to Canada from Venray near the Belgian Border in 1922. Her breakfasts were to die for. We had pea meal bacon, two eggs easy over, alongside a stack of steaming, fluffy pancakes swathed in butter and doused with maple syrup under a generous sprinkling of cinnamon and brown sugar. In my letters from home mum was complaining about rationed breakfast cereal, a couple of rashers of bacon a week and having to use powdered milk in her so-called cup of coffee made with chicory or dandelion root instead of the real thing.

After breakfast I walked through the park to the river. It was so wide, even so far inland, miles from the coast. It made the Teviot look like a burn and the Slitrig a trickle. The noise of the birds was strange too. At Moncton I rarely noticed the birds but here the whistles of the bright red cardinals and the harsh grating of the grackles made the place seem incredibly foreign. I headed east along the river to the Downtown area. The architecture was stunning. There were so many churches including the awe-inspiring tower of Christ Church Cathedral, which Mrs De Kuyper later told me was North America's first cathedral. As well as the churches there were the public buildings built by settlers who were clearly proud of their new land. Everything was bigger, much bigger than Hawick. I was struck by the Legislative Assembly building but underwhelmed by the City Hall. The latter was a three-storey, red brick construction, a bright green roof and gold-coloured architectural detail. Compared with the four-storey magnificence of the Hawick Town Hall, constructed in the Scottish Baronial style with its imposing clocktower, Fredericton's city fathers were evidently not as well thought of as the burgesses of Hawick. After about an hour of wandering around I found myself outside the Beaverbrook Art Gallery. I had been good at art at school and our art mistress, Miss Redpath, was a great enthusiast, showing us her collection of prints of paintings by the great masters. Obviously in Hawick where there was no art gallery we never got the chance to look at original paintings. I wondered what I would find and how I would react. The sculptures outside certainly were inviting. Once inside I went to the desk and was immediately welcomed like a long lost friend. I was in uniform and the attendant waived the entrance fee and made embarrassing noises about how grateful she was for the sacrifices we were making as part of the war effort. She told me to start in gallery 1.

For the next hour and a half I was transported to heaven. The collection included paintings by Thomas Gainsborough, John Constable, J.M.W. Turner and Joshua Reynolds amongst others. I was stunned and dumbfounded. There was a magic in these galleries that I had never experienced before. Miss Redpath would be jealous when I told her what I had seen when I eventually got home.

By now I was getting a wee bit hungry. Mrs De Kuyper told me I just had to go to a coffee house to experience the real Canada. There was a coffee house five minutes away on King Street. By the time I had turned right off St John's Street I could detect the faint aroma of freshly brewed coffee. As instructed by Mrs De Kuyper I ordered a double-double and a bagel with cream cheese. I went over to the far side of the restaurant and sat down at an empty table.

Over the hubbub of conversing diners there were the familiar tones of distinctive Hawick accents. I turned round and could not believe what I saw. I said, 'Pietro and Bianca what the hell are you doing here'? They did not respond. I did a double take. It was definitely them.

I raised my voice. 'Pietro and Bianca what on earth are you doing here?' They both turned and looked up. Their expressions of amazement slowly morphed into smiles. We all got up and in the middle of a restaurant full of people getting their lunch. I gave Pietro an enormous bear hug. Bianca soon joined in and I was conscious of her firm breasts and pubic bone pressing into my right thigh. We all started laughing together. Tears streamed down the Carlucci siblings' cheeks. We stood back in silence and stared at each other. Then Pietro rather strangely said, 'can we join you'? There were three empty seats at my table and Pietro and Bianca brought their coffees over and sat down.

We all started talking at once.

Bianca: 'I see you are in uniform. Are you based here'?

Me: 'I thought you were at Stobs. How come you are in Canada'?

Pietro: 'We'd heard you had been shot down and badly injured. Have they sent you here to recover'?

I had recently been promoted to pilot officer. I was feeling full of myself and found it had made me more confident so I said, 'Shhhh we can't all talk over each other. I'll go first'. They both smiled and Bianca put her arm out and held my hand.

She said, 'okay, but it's so good to see you'.

'When I joined up I trained to be a pilot. I passed out with flying colours. Instead of sending me to a squadron to fight the Luftwaffe they said I would be more use teaching new recruits to fly. I was sent on a special course for flight instructors in Wales and then transferred to Moncton where we can train new pilots to fly without risk of being attacked by the enemy. I have been in Canada for ages and this is my first spell of leave'.

Pietro took up his story, 'one day the family were arrested under the Emergency Powers Act, 1939, Section 18b. We were being detained because we were enemy aliens. We appeared at a tribunal in Gala and our parents, being Italian born were sentenced to confinement in Stobs camp which had been converted as an internment camp for enemy aliens from Germany and Italy. Because Bianca and I had been born in Scotland they gave us the choice of being interred with our parents or joining up as part of the British war effort. It was a really difficult decision. We felt Scottish but we did not want to be separated from mama and papa. So we chose to go to Stobs - it was almost like staying at home but a lot tougher. After a while they decided they wanted Stobs to become an army training camp for the Coldstream Guards and KOSBs. We might have been sent to the Isle of Man but instead we were put on a ship to Canada and ended up in Camp B/70 near here'.

Bianca took up her story, 'you are probably wondering what we are doing wandering about downtown Fredericton without a guard. Well to cut a long story short I was persuaded to help the Royal Canadian Mounted Police. I was effectively sent under cover and information I gathered enabled them to arrest a group of terrorist and fascist sympathisers who were bringing arms and explosives into Canada. My reward was being allowed to spend every Saturday with Pietro or the parents in Moncton instead of being locked in our hut at the camp. The Mounties also give me $5.00 so we can eat in places like this or go to the cinema if it's raining or snowing'.

I asked, 'how long have you got today'?

Bianca answered, 'the truck picks us up at 5 o'clock so we have until then to catch up. It really is great to see you again. We will need to meet up earlier next Saturday so we can spend more time together'.

I felt my first twinge of sadness. 'That's not possible. I have got to leave to go back to Moncton on Friday. Can you come into town during the week'?

'No. That's not possible replied Bianca. 'We work in the forest near Lake Killarney everyday so we'll just have to make do with what's left of the afternoon'.

With that I was overcome by sadness and a pleasantly agonising feeling of nostalgia. We had only been together for ten minutes or so and I had this overwhelming sense of home sickness gnawing away in the pit of my stomach. It really was a wonderful and a totally unexpected surprise to bump into the Carluccis again. Pietro hadn't really changed but Bianca had. She was now a very attractive woman and not the schoolgirl I remembered. She had filled out in all the right places. Her perfect round face had a healthy tan showing off her radiant smile, which emitted an infectious laugh that quickly evolved into a self-conscious giggle. She was lovely.

Pietro said, 'have you been to Queen's Square or Rabbit-town? That would be a lovely walk and give you a chance to learn a bit about Fredericton's history. There are lots of interesting historic buildings and shops in Rabbit-town'.

I asked, 'why is it called Rabbit-town'?

Pietro was always good at history at school. 'Apparently it acquired its name sometime in the early 1900's. Writings by the true Rabbit Towners say that the name came from their trapping of rabbits in the area then "back of town" for food and for the skins. Its not true what they say about trappers only being interested in beaver and bear pelts'.

When we finished our coffees, which were really rather good, we headed off to Rabbit-town but we never got there. The sun was high in the sky. It was hot and humid. When we got to Queen's Square there was a large sequoia tree casting a cooling shadow over a bench at the foot of its trunk. Sequoias are natives of the west coast, from British Columbia to California. This mature specimen had been planted some time ago by one of the leading families in New Brunswick. The tree gave off a musky, resinous scent and the shade it provided was a welcome relief on such a warm afternoon. We three Borderers had never experienced the like at home. We spent all afternoon talking and laughing on that bench.

We covered every topic under the sun and the afternoon flew by. Ever since they had been taken away from Stobs the Carluccis had been starved of news from home. Pietro asked if I got letters from Rubers Hill and what was the news'? I told him about the rationing and war time privations experienced by everyone in and around Hawick. I told Pietro that the rugby club had been put into mothballs for the duration. Most of the players had been called up or had volunteered to fight. There were only young boys and older men available to play. In addition, the schools stopped playing rugby because there were no male coaches to supervise games and teach the boys the basics. One or two of the female teachers tried to fill the breach but they weren't very good. There was the occasional friendly game when two teams could be put together. The posts stayed up at Mansfield Park continuing their vigil of towering over the men in green who continued to represent the town regardless. In one letter from Dad - he rarely wrote to me, it was usually Mum - he mentioned that a former England Internationalist, who was an officer billeted at Stobs, donned the famous green jersey and played for Hawick. He was quick and scored a try down at the sewage work's end.

Mum's letters were mainly about families, sons and fathers who had been killed or injured or who had been captured and languished in PoW camps on the continent. She also wrote a lot about farming. In one sense that hadn't changed much because farming was a reserved occupation. Even so she said that a squad of land girls had been billeted around the district to help with the lambing and shearing. One, a rather blousy girl, had caused a bit of a scandal because, allegedly, she had been caught in the vestry with the minister. I doubt whether that was true knowing how straight-laced the Rev. McCall was. Mum told me that Mrs McCall was ashamed to show her face in the shops in town.

'Not much has changed then,' said Pietro. 'In the camp we are absolutely starved of news of what is going on in the outside world. One of the inmates in the next hut built a crystal set radio by having parts smuggled in by a bribable guard. Sadly it was soon found during a routine search and was confiscated. Even then when Herr Rundveld shared what he heard it wasn't very interesting. Being a fascist sympathiser Rundveld tuned into shortwave radio stations which broadcast reports about how the armies of the third reich were making progress in eastern Europe. We weren't sure if we could believe him'.

'You were right not to believe him. I listen to the BBC World Service and I get official bulletins now and again from RAF Cranwell. I can tell you that the Allies have landed in France and that there is a large detachment of the Canadian Army in Normandy as part of the big push to Berlin. It's hard going and only recently a German U-boat torpedoed HMCS Magog not far from here in the St Lawrence. The Magog went down and three sailors were killed. Overall though I think it is going well, certainly far better than in the early days of the war. I think the Jerries will sue for peace next year or in 1946 if things carry on as they are'.

'Let's stop this talk of war', interrupted Bianca. 'I am so happy we are together again. Let's relive the old days,'

'I don't think we can do that', observed Pietro. 'We are all older now. We have been through a lot and we might never see Skelfhill Pen or the Eildon Hills again. We are lucky to be alive, the three of us together on a lovely day in this idyllic spot under this magnificent tree'. The rest of the afternoon flew by in a reverie of reminiscence. When Pietro heard the bell of the City Hall clock chime the half hour he said, 'good grief, it's half past four. We are going to have to scoot to meet the truck to take us back to camp'.

I felt sad for the second time this afternoon. Over the past few hours I had felt a growing feeling of warmth and attraction towards Bianca and I was sure that my feelings were reciprocated. I was correct. Bianca said it was a shame that we might not see each other for a long time. She came up with a devious plan for a secret assignation on the coming Wednesday.

While we had been seated on the bench Bianca told me all about Claudio Houde and how she and he used to meet up in an isolated cottage which was used to store caches of weapons and explosives. Apparently the RCMP had locked it up and it lay empty at the end of a narrow animal track, the entrance of which was hidden off one of the many trails through the forest.

On Wednesday morning I set off early from the B&B. I had got a map from Parks Canada which clearly showed the trail I had to follow. Bianca told me after about a mile to look out for the animal trail on the left. She said it was difficult to spot and that I should look out for some damage on the branches of a tree where deer had been rubbing their antlers. She said it was also a fox scenting area and their distinctive scent was exactly the same as Scottish foxes. I found the trail without too much trouble. It was covered in broken branches after a recent storm. There was an eerie silence disturbed occasionally by the chittering of chipmunks which were to be seen scurrying through the undergrowth. After about a quarter of an hour I came upon a clearing with a rather ramshackle cottage which might be better described as a cabin. There were three pines at the back just as Bianca had described. The RCMP had locked up the dwelling. Their distinctive badge with a buffalo's head under a crown stood with its motto, *Maintiens le Droit* next to a sign that said, 'Warning Keep Out'. There were planks nailed across the doors and windows but they had left a rocking chair and wooden bench with a threadbare cushion on the patio. I settled myself down, opened a bottle of Pepsi and waited to see if Bianca had managed to escape the attention of the guards. I did not have long to wait.

Bianca appeared at the edge of the clearing. She was carrying her work coverall over her arm and holding her work gloves in her hands. There were signs she had tried to spruce up before meeting me. Her grey prison blouse with a large red circle on the back was tucked into her denim skirt, emphasising her femininity. Her hair was a bit limp but I guessed internees were not blessed with supplies of shampoo. I thought she looked lovely.

I stood up and walked down the step and stood and looked at her for what seemed like an age. When she suggested we meet like this last Saturday I knew that our relationship had changed. With the sun in her face Bianca screwed up her eyes, a move that seemed to highlight her freckles. She was smiling to herself and at me. We moved slowly towards each other, opened our arms and pressed together in a tender embrace. We stood like that for another age. Then we both started talking at once. We knew that something was different for us.

Bianca told me that once she got back to the camp on Saturday evening she had not stopped thinking about me. I told her that it was the same for me and that every morning since, I had gone back to Queen's Square and sat on the same bench under the sequoia we had sat upon on Saturday.

Hand in hand we walked back together to the verandah and sat with our arms around each other on the top step. Ever the practical one, even with her mind in its current distracted state, Bianca said, 'I haven't got long. I'll be missed and the guards will start looking for me. I've got a friend to cover for me and to say I have had to take myself off into the bushes if the guards ask questions. I had to promise her that I wouldn't be more than an hour'. She turned her head looked up and kissed me. I had never had a girl's tongue in my mouth before and the feeling was more exciting than the first time I had looped the loop. I knew that I was in love.

With so little time together and little or no opportunity of seeing each other soon we agreed to write to each other. Most of the other guys back at the station got love letters from their girls. Until now I only got letters from my mother.

*   *   *

RCAF Moncton

October 1944

My Darling Bianca,

I have been back in the station for two weeks now and there is an enormous hole in my life. – you are not with me.

I could not have believed my luck when I bumped into you and Pietro in the Coffee House in Fredericton. Chance encounters like that only happen in books but for us it was real.

Life here is even more monotonous than usual. I no longer get the same buzz out of flying and some of the young trainee pilots are inept. I could tell you more about what I am doing and about the encouraging news from the front in Europe. I can't say more because it won't pass the censor.

I miss you so much and can't wait to hear from you. I understand there are restrictions on internees sending though not receiving letters. Please write as soon as you can. I miss you dreadfully.

All my love

Your Very Own Hughie
X X X X X

Three months later I got a reply..

Camp B/70

January 1945

My Love

After Christmas the RCMP, who intercepted and read your letter, granted me permission to write to you. They said you were the right sort.

Like you I miss you dreadfully. I can never stop thinking about you.

Life goes on as before. Pietro and I are at last getting acclimatised to the searing cold and snow. The authorities have given us new warmer parkas this year. They are a big help but hopeless when it ncomes to ice pellets striking your face when we are out in the woods. The ice and snow actually make it easier to move the timber as it slides more easily over the ground. There is no clatchy mud for it to get stuck in. But you don't want to hear about our work. Like it is for you life is monotonous and I can't wait for the war to end so we can see each other again.

Write soon

Your love Bianca

XXXXXXXXXXX

We continued to exchange letters. After VE Day our lives were to change for ever.

Chapter 11   Bianca

1945 - Fredericton NB & Ottawa ON

It was the middle of June. Just after breakfast in the mess one of the guards who continued to be unpleasant to everyone, especially the Germans, even though the war had ended appeared at the door and yelled, 'family Carlucci, all of you, report to the Mounties' office at ten hundred hours sharp'. He clicked his heels, turned sharp about and marched off without a word of explanation.

'I wonder what all that is about', murmured Mum and Dad in unison.

At ten on the dot Dad knocked on the Mounties' door. It was opened and we were greeted by a moustachioed RCMP officer. 'I'm Inspector McClintock. Come in and take a seat there in front of my desk'. I must say we were all overawed and a little apprehensive. The inspector turned towards me and addressed me directly, 'Miss Carlucci you were very helpful to us a while back. You were very brave and winkled out information that allowed us to take action to prevent an attack on the Dominion of Canada. We were able to put an end to a well-used arms smuggling route. Our enemies were imprisoned in Kingston and they will stay there for a long time. We are ever so grateful for your actions'. He paused. 'I am very pleased to say that the Governor General of Canada has instructed me to advise you that he wishes to present you with a medal for bravery in Ottawa later this year'.

There was a collective gasp of amazement on our side of the desk.

'What's more,' continued the inspector. 'I am well aware that my colleagues made a number of promises to you when you agreed to act undercover on our behalf. If you remember we said we would offer you either full Canadian citizenship plus help with starting a new life or free passage back to Scotland in a good deal more comfort than you experienced on your way over. We intend to keep our promise'. He paused. 'You don't need to make up your minds now but I would like to know what you would like to do in the next couple of weeks. Now, it only remains for me to officially thank you on behalf of the Canadian Government'. At that he extended his arms, kissed me on both cheeks, shook Dad's, Mum's and Pietro's hands, saluted and escorted us out of the door.

It was a warm and sunny day in more ways than one. We meandered around the compound and left the camp through the now unguarded gate. We wandered down the road to Gagetown and Minto. Seeing the name Minto on the sign made us all feel nostalgic. Minto had obviously been settled by immigrants from Minto, a village only a few miles over the hills from Bonchester Bridge. 'Oh, I want to go home', said Mum. 'I can already taste the sea trout your father used to catch on their annual spawning run up the Rule Water'.

'I'm not so sure' said Dad, 'though the taste of trout makes my mouth water. It's so much tastier than the pickerel you get here'. I thought I saw him salivating. 'We have got to take our time. This is a big decision.

Do we stay together as a family in Canada or Scotland or do we split up and go our separate ways'?

I was conflicted. I wanted us to stay together, yet I wanted to be with Hughie. After a successful career in the RAF, he had now been promoted to Flight Lieutenant. I couldn't see him wanting to go back to farming at Rubers Hill. Pietro was the same age as Hughie and I couldn't see him having a passionate desire to return to Bonchester Bridge either. Mum and Dad were different. They had taken a big risk in walking to Scotland from Italy with the Padrone all those years ago in the pursuit of a better life. It had been a struggle but they had set up a business which was thriving when the war came along. The business would have been confiscated and I wonder if they would want to start again in Scotland or to make changes here in Canada.

That evening we had what the local Mi'kmaqs would have called a pow wow. Dad took us all down to Dino's Diner, a restaurant which served food masquerading as Italian, on the outskirts of Fredericton. We had decent pasta with a flavourful ragu served with a pleasant local wine. Dad took charge and said, 'we have got some serious decision making ahead of us and I would like us to come to a family decision and I really hope it suits us all. I suggest that each of us speaks without interruption saying what we think and then we chew it all over together'. He smiled and said, 'I'm sure we won't come to blows. Mama you start '.

I had never heard Mum be so philosophical before. She started back in Barga, where she lived in a two-room rural cottage with an earthen floor. 'When Papa told me one day that he wanted to better himself and that he had spoken to the Padrone who was taking a small group across the Alps, through France and over the sea to Scotland I was devastated. I didn't want to go but he was my husband and I had solemnly promised to obey him till death do us part. When we got to Bonchester Bridge I was so unhappy. It was very, very cold and it never seemed to stop raining. I couldn't speak the language. I walked down a strange street and heard the voices of strangers and thought about my family and loved ones back home. I felt desperately alone. Once I felt so homesick that my heart pounded and I burst into tears. I felt ashamed crying out in the open opposite the Horse and Hounds but I had no one to talk to. I had no one I could pour my heart out to. Eventually my English got better. Dad's business did well and the locals appreciated what he had to sell. I never really made friends but I had my bambini. Then the war came along and the authorities arrested us as enemy aliens - that was a joke. But no; we spent a miserable time in Stobs and then they sent us here and we had to wear these prison clothes'. She looked up out of the window. 'I am not sure where I belong and I still feel homesick for the old country. I guess I don't want to go back to Scotland. They rejected us and the Canadians appear to want us to stay. It would mean starting afresh again but my vote is that we should stay on this side of the Atlantic'.

Pietro, when his turn came, was direct and to the point. 'My future lies in the New World. There are far more opportunities for me here. I would only miss playing rugby and I haven't played a game for the last umpteen years. My vote is to stay'.

Mum's and Pietro's desire to stay in Canada didn't really make it any easier for me. I still wanted to stay together with the family but I also wanted to create a new family with Hughie. What was he going to do? Would he be demobbed back in Hawick or would his tour in Canada be extended after the war and might I be able to persuade him to stay with me. I knew in my heart that he was in love with me and would want to get married. I also knew that I would have to follow the example of Mum and go wherever my man goes. My mind was all of a jumble so I said to the others. 'I am on the horns of a dilemma. I want to stay as part of this family but I also want to be with Hughie and I don't know what he will be doing after the war or where he will live'.

'Well that's honest' said Dad. 'When you can you'll have to find out what his plans are. Listening to the three of you says wonders about the strengths and bonds of this far-travelled branch of the Carlucci family. It is clear that I should tell the Inspector that we want to stay here and what plans does he have for us? Where will we go? What can we do'? At that he ordered another bottle of wine and we spent the rest of the evening reminiscing about Scotland and Italy as well as dreaming aloud about what we might do next. The following morning Dad and Mum took themselves off to the Mounties' office.

Mr Carlucci knocked at the door.

'Come in'.

'Good morning Inspector.'

'Good morning Mr and Mrs Carlucci.' This was the first time my parents had ever been addressed using Mr and Mrs and not just their surnames. We also had enemy aliens' internee numbers but these were only used in documents. 'Well, I guess you have come to a decision'. Dad nodded. 'That's quick. What would you like to do'?

My father gave a one word reply, 'stay'.

'Well that's just great. We need hard-working people like you, especially to help with postwar reconstruction'.

'I am not very good at building work,' responded my father.

'That's not what I meant. We need good people and families like yours all over the country to do all sorts of things. We already have something in mind which we think will suit you down to the ground'. My father looked relieved and said, 'what's that'?

'Well first of all we will send you to our capital city, Ottawa. That makes sense because it is there where Bianca will be invited to go to Rideau Hall to be presented with her bravery medal by the Earl of Athlone, the Governor General. I have had a look at what you did before the war and we think you would do well running a shop in the Little Italy district. All the family could work there and eventually, if they wanted, Pietro and Bianca could find work elsewhere. There is a big demand for labour in Ontario, indeed in most of Canada'.

The Inspector did not waste his time and the following week we all gathered together what few possessions we had, donned our new civilian clothes and set off for Ottawa. We first travelled on a bus to Quebec City. It was a long journey taking over eight hours. Quebec City was a bit like a fairy tale. It was set on the St Lawrence River which, even though it was narrower there, was still unbelievably wide. Quebec City sat on top of cliffs with the towering Château Frontenac Hotel and imposing Citadelle of Quebec dominating the skyline. Sadly we did not have time to do any sight seeing. We were taken straight to the railway station for our onward journey. The first thing we noticed was that everyone spoke French. In New Brunswick we noticed that some of the signs were in English and French but we rarely heard anyone speak anything other than English, albeit with a North American accent. The way people spoke was quite infectious and even after a short time we started saying padio instead of patio and pants instead of trousers.

The Mounties had given us some Canadian dollars and vouchers for our meals. We found a restaurant and ordered a chicken sandwich. It was like a sandwich we had never had before being served with chips or fries or frites as they are called here with a salad of lettuce and tomato on the side. It was served with iced water. After years of eating in the camp canteen it was a meal fit for the king. Feeling full we made our way to the Gare du Palais and caught the CPR, Canadian Pacific Railway, train to Ottawa. After an hour's stop in Montreal, where everybody also spoke French, our eight hour journey ended at Ottawa Train Station not far from the Downtown core. We were met by a Mounty constable and a smart young woman wearing a crisply pressed skirt and matching jacket and looking as if she had walked straight out of an Eaton's catalogue. They were carrying a cardboard sign with "CARLUCCI FAMILY" written on it.

'Welcome to Ottawa', said the young lady. You must be tired after your long journey. Let me take your pack. My name is Anne Field and this is Constable Deline. We are here to take you to your new home and shop and to help you get settled in. We have a car over here'.

That night we slept like logs in a sparsely furnished apartment over an empty shop which was situated next to a trattoria and gelato parlour in Preston Street. When we arrived there Anne said that they would give us a couple of days to rest up and familiarise ourselves with the area and then come back to help us set up the business. She gave us some more money, as she said, to tide us by, nothing was too much for such a brave and heroic family.

The following day we woke bright and early and couldn't wait to explore our new home. Preston Street was long and straight. It was busy and bustling and a far cry from Bonchester Bridge. There were a fair number of families of Italian extraction, some of whom had been released from internment camps just like us. Other families had been there several generations and avoided being interned for the duration. One of the things that surprised me was the number of people from different places and different ethnicities. Until then I had never seen Chinese people before. China Town with its strange arches, lanterns and dragons was situated nearby.

After breakfast of coffee and bread rolls we headed off north up Preston Street. There were lots of cafés, bakers, grocers, a shoe shop, a hardware store, a gas station, a garage, and a dentist with a giant tooth on an advertising sign outside. There were also numerous pubs and bars. At the end of the street or Preston as the locals called it, was a lovely park and an enormous lake. Dows Lake had apparently been built to a accommodate felled tree trunks being floated down river to hungry paper mills. These days there were only a few people paddling canoes for fun while navigating several flocks of Canada geese. Everywhere we went people were smiling and in a coffee shop we got talking to an enthusiastic local who told us in the winter the lake froze over and people would be out skating and having impromptu games of hockey. Our new friend explained the lake was joined to the Rideau Canal which ran all the way from Ottawa to Kingston on Lake Ontario where Claudio was imprisoned.

After a couple of days Anne Field arrived with an official from the Canadian immigration authorities. The official was a middle-ranking field officer. He was wearing a double breasted suit that had seen better days. His trousers had baggy knees and the seat of his pants resembled a dirty mirror. His scruffiness was offset by a bow tie with a red maple leaf pattern on a white background. Between his fingers he held a cigarette with about a quarter of an inch of ash balanced precariously on the end. In spite of initial impressions he was a pleasant enough chap and seemed to know his job. Above all he was helpful.

As a family we were still a bit disoriented. After all we had been through a period of an immense change in our circumstances in a very short time, with no opportunity to acclimatise or adjust. Mr Goodman, the man from the ministry seemed to recognise this. He explained that he and his department were here to help us and he made a great fuss about the service that I had performed for the country by preventing a terrorist attack. We were told that the Federal Government would provide us with a grant to help to get us started and to tide us over for the first four weeks. After that, provided Dad could come up with a sound business plan, the government would provide us with loan finance with a low interest payment to get the business up and running. We were told that the shop premises and the apartment above would be provided rent-free for three months. He also left us with clothing vouchers to spend in the Hudson Bay Company shop in Sparks Street. I was told to make sure I bought a pretty frock, matching coat, hat and gloves to wear when I went to Rideau Hall for my medal ceremony.

At the start of the meeting with Miss Field and Mr Goodman we were all a trifle apprehensive, but by the end we could not believe Canada's generosity. We had well and truly landed on our feet. Even so Mr Goodman warned us that life would involve hard work. It was not easy to set up a new business from scratch in a new city in an unfamiliar country. He told us that Canada was a land of immigrants from many different countries and that we should expect to be made welcome but to keep our feet on the ground as we would inevitably face unexpected problems.

After the officials had gone Dad summed up the morning by saying what nice people they were, how welcome they had made us and that they had given us an unbelievable financial leg up to build a new life. Over lunch he behaved a bit like a big shot business executive allocating us tasks and a time table that we had to stick to. His aim was to produce a business plan that would impress Mr Goodman so that we would get that business loan he told us about. For the next couple of weeks Pietro and I tramped the streets within a couple of miles radius of where we lived. It was up and down Preston from Carling to Somerset Street. We also ranged from Bronson to Wellington. Our purpose was to see what potential rival shops there were, what they sold and perhaps more importantly what they didn't sell. We were surprised to find that in Little Italy and its immediate neighbourhoods there was not a shop that sold Italian food for consumption at home. You could get pasta and products like focaccia, grissini and coffee for espresso in restaurants but not for consuming at home. Dad was convinced we had found a niche market and set about creating a business plan for Carlucci's Italian Delicatessen. The plan was dependent on getting supplies of produce. Importing foodstuffs from Italy was out of the question so we sought out specialist local suppliers of durum wheat for making our own fresh pasta as well as cured meats, olive oils and mediterranean-type vegetables. By chance we came across an interesting wholesale business in ByWard Market. It could supply us with oils and dry goods. By sheer chance we also found an Italian butcher, who produced salami and other cured meats, in Mississauga near Toronto where a large number of people who came from Italy lived. Fortunately there was a good regular train service so we could be assured of a daily supply of fresh produce. We also found a greengrocer in Mississauga who sourced vegetables like tomatoes, zuccini, aubergines and arborio rice from a company in California. We had our supply chain sorted and Mr Goodman and his colleagues duly approved our business plan. They issued the loan and two and half months after we arrived in Ottawa Carlucci's Italian Delicatessen was opened for business.

All the while I was so busy I did not mope around missing Hughie, though he was rarely far from my thoughts. A week after the deli opened I got a letter which had been forwarded from Camp B/70 in Fredericton. It was from Hughie.

RCAF Moncton

October 1945

My Darling Bianca,

It has been ages since I have heard from you. I have been so unhappy not hearing from you but I know it is difficult to write from the camp.

I continue to get regular letters from home and Mum says they will be throwing a big party for my return. She tells me that Stobs is being shut down and that Dad bought one of the old huts - the MoD was selling them for agricultural use. Apparently little has changed in Bonchester Bridge and Mum said that old Aggie Smith who used to live next door to you is looking forward to seeing you back. I understand she has been looking after your horse, which because of its age, has been put out to grass.

The war in Europe and Japan is over and there is talk of our demobilisation. I guess you will be returning eventually to Scotland and you must let me know when as I can't wait to see you again. Sadly that will not happen as soon as I would have hoped as the other day my commanding officer said that my demob papers had been delayed and that I was being transferred to work in the British High Commission in Ottawa to help with the resettlement of British children who had been evacuated to Canada during the war. So, sadly, getting together and holding you in my arms again is going to be delayed.

Please write soon. I will be here until just after Christmas and I will send you my new address in Ottawa.

I can't wait until I see you again.

All my love

Your Very Own Hughie
X X X X X

I had to read the letter again and again. I could not believe it. I had never been happier in my life. Hughie was coming to live and work in Ottawa in a few weeks. Should I write and let him know I was here already or should I wait and surprise him. I knew where the British High Commission was. It was that building with the Union Jack flying above it on Elgin Street. I passed it on my way to ByWard Market to visit the wholesalers.

Chapter 12 Hughie

1946 - Ottawa ON

The last year had been a hectic one. During the first half of the year there had been a rush on training more and more pilots to support the push on from the Normandy beaches after D Day. We were also working to hasten the end of the war in Japan. No one had anticipated Hiroshima and the speedy end to hostilities. After the celebrations there was the hard graft of rowing back on all the activities and cutting back personnel and support services on the station. Excitement was always in the air with the thought of demobilisation, going home and seeing Bianca again.

All that came to an end shortly after VJ Day when the station commander said that I was going to be posted to the British High Commission in Ottawa. I was being sent there to work as an Admin Officer Grade A with my pay going up by $10 per month. My job was to help with the resettlement of British children who had been evacuated to Canada as a precaution against German bombing at home. Most of the kids apparently came from the big cities, London, Birmingham, Manchester and Newcastle. I said I knew nothing about administration or how to go about the job. I was an RAF officer and flying instructor. 'Excellent background', was the CO's response. 'Just think of all the admin you have to do with that job. You were always complaining to me about the paperwork.

You'll be all right and you are good at managing and motivating people, and that will be a big part of your new job'. The squadron leader reassured me that I would get training on the job. He also pointed out that it was no accident that an officer from RCAF Moncton had been selected. During the war the CBC had been working with the BBC to set up experimental transatlantic radio links allowing child evacuees in Canada to talk to their parents in England. There was a lot of experience locally that I could tap into and I could spend some of my time getting to know the children and the young people involved.

I met the CBC producer a couple of days after I had been informed of my new posting. He told me that at the beginning of the War there were realistic fears about possible invasion as well as bombing. As early as 1939, children in urban centres were evacuated to the countryside for their safety. 'Operation Pied Piper' moved approximately three million children across Britain and around the world to Commonwealth or allied countries. I was told that up to 10,000 children came to Canada either through government schemes or privately. There would have been more children but Churchill shut down the Canadian relocation programme after 77 children perished when a German submarine torpedoed the SS City of Benares en route to Canada. My CBC mentor turned out to be a godsend. When I started work in Ottawa I was much better prepared than I feared and I found out the squadron leader was right when he said that I would take admin in my stride. In the end I worked for nine months running the child relocation programme in Ottawa. It was the most rewarding and satisfying work experience of my life.

Initially, separating children from their parents was traumatic for all concerned. Most of the children were homesick and very unhappy. When they arrived in Canada they were often made to line up against a wall so that prospective surrogate parents or hosts, as they were called, could take their pick. The good looking children were usually the first chosen and some of the more insensitive adults said, 'I'll take that one'. It was not a propitious start for the children, who had already been traumatised by being separated from their parents and who had suffered from sea sickness during the voyage. My job was to identify where the children were and match them up with the location of their parents, indeed, checking that they were still alive, in Britain. That in itself was a large task. I was told to concentrate on the Canadian end and to leave linking the kids to their real parents to the ministry in London as well as organisations like the Women's Voluntary Service and Citizens Advice Bureaux. Mine was no small task as the children had been housed all over Canada, though most of them were in the Maritimes and Ontario.

The children on the whole were very excited about the prospect of going home. They had all been in Canada for a number of years and had adjusted to the North American way of life. Many, especially the younger ones, had become attached to their adoptive parents. They were forced to experience separation anxiety for the second time in their short lives. Not all of the children, however, wanted to go home to Britain. One seventeen-year-old girl billeted in Moncton had grown particularly fond of her adoptive parents. She was a very intelligent girl and won a place to study history at one of Canada's oldest universities, Dalhousie, in Halifax Nova Scotia. This led me to being involved in a prolonged correspondence with both her birth and adoptive parents. In the end it was decided she should go to university here and go and see her parents at the end of her three year course. I never found out what happened to her though rumour says she became a professor.

I also had to find chaperones to accompany groups of children on the voyage home. That was a difficult task. Young women tended to want to stay in Canada. The idea of travelling to a war-torn Britain still suffering from food and fuel rationing did not appeal to many. Another problem was finding berths for the children. So much shipping had been sunk during the war or converted into being troop ships and cargo ships. On top of that there were thousand of troops, refugees or displaced persons needing transport to take them home or to pastures new. In reality this part of my job was not as difficult as I feared. Shipping was packed to the gunnels with passengers travelling from Europe to North America. Demand to go in the opposite direction was not nearly so high. Fortunately I managed to negotiate some good deals with shipping lines keen to earn ticket money on the route back to Europe to pick up more passengers to sail west again.

One day, not long after my arrival in Ottawa, I had a phone call from the sergeant manning the reception desk in the front lobby, 'Sir, there is some one here to to see you. Could you come downstairs as she is not cleared for me to give her a pass to come in'. I straightened my tie and made sure that the buttons on my tunic were fastened. I wondered who it was. I was feeling pretty chipper as I had just managed to sign up three new chaperones. I left the warmth of my office and went down the stone stairs at the end of the building. The outside wall was nearly all window. I could see the snowy wastes outside and people skating on the Rideau Canal which fell away through a series of locks to the Ottawa River below. I don't know why but I started whistling Vera Lynn's *We'll meet again.* I skipped down four storeys, opened the half glass door into Reception and couldn't believe my eyes. I abandoned all protocol and dashed over to Bianca, threw my arms around her and engaged in what must have been the longest kiss ever witnessed in a British High Commission office. And, being in Reception in full view of Elgin Street our embrace must have been witnessed by dozens of people, but neither of us cared.

Eventually we drew back and looked at each other, eyes locked together. We both had big broad grins on our faces. I was even shaking a little. This was an unbelievable experience. I could hardly get my words out and muttered, 'what are you doing here'? She replied, 'and what are you doing here? Actually I know, because you wrote and told me you had been posted to Ottawa. I live with Mum, Dad and Pietro in Little

Italy above a delicatessen business we run. We were sent here by the Canadian government. Remember I told you about how I was asked to spy for the Mounties well this is sort of their reward and I am getting a medal from the Governor General'. The words came tumbling out,' I missed you so much. Life was empty without you, even with so much going on. When we were released from the camp and moved here and got settled in and started the shop and I have learned how to make pasta which we sell and . . . oh I have so much I want to tell you and I want to find out what you have been up to and what are your plans'? She did not stop to draw breath, 'I suppose you are working and can't get away now. What about lunch'?

I eventually found my voice, 'yes. Lunch is a good idea. There's a pub round the corner in Sparks Street'.

She laughed. 'You can tell you are new to these parts. Women, especially respectable women, are not welcome in Ottawa pubs. Haven't you seen there are two doors into the pub and one is marked "Gentlemen" and the other "Women & Escorts"'.

I replied, 'I didn't know that. This is such a special occasion we'll push the boat out. I'll take you to the Chateau Laurier. Can you meet me here at half past twelve. I'll skive off for the afternoon'. She nodded, lent forward to kiss me on the lips and turned smiling over her shoulder. 'See you later. I love you'. I walked slowly up the stairs in a daze and went back to my desk. I could not concentrate and the minute hand never moved more slowly round the clock. It eventually got to 12.25. I put my fur hat and great coat on and ran down the stairs at top speed.

The Chateau Laurier was the place to go in Ottawa if not in all Canada. Fortunately I had just been paid but even so I experienced a smirr of concern that I might not have enough money. I thought, who cares? The Chateau Laurier was a fairy-tale castle of a place ten storeys high under magical towers and green copper roofs. It was just over the way from the High Commission, next to where the Rideau Canal joined the Ottawa River and opposite the parliament buildings. It was the haunt of Hollywood stars and leading politicians. One of the most famous photographs of Churchill was on display in the hotel and was a place of pilgrimage for many. The photo known as the *Roaring Lion* was taken in 1941 after Churchill had given a wartime speech to Canada's House of Commons. For many of the visitors to the hotel the scowl captured on Churchill's face came to symbolise British resolve against the Nazis.

The large double doors were opened for us by a liveried doorman who ushered us into a large bar area with enormous leather chairs and mahogany tables with polished brass ornamentation. After a cocktail we had a four course lunch with all the trimmings, washed down with coffee and liqueurs. I felt replete and very, very, happy. We talked and talked. Neither of us could believe our luck that after all these years fate had decided we should end up in the same town.

The next couple of months flew by and the weather began to get a bit warmer, I spent lots of time with Bianca and the Carluccis and was so pleased to see that their business was thriving. Only a few days after our long lunch at the Chateau Laurier I proposed and was accepted. We set a date in May. Bianca often came round to my place although she never spent the night. She wanted to save herself. I had an apartment in Westboro which wasn't too far from Little Italy. We went for walks together round the area down to the river and I taught Bianca to skate on a rink that was in a local park and used by the kids for hockey games. I had learned to skate in New Brunswick and taught Bianca the elements of gliding, stopping and turning by using an old metal chair to keep her balance. She was a natural and it wasn't long before we both felt confident enough to join the families and lovers skating on the Rideau Canal. Weekends there were special with stalls at the edge of the ice selling hot drinks, frozen maple syrup and delicious beavertails.

During the week Bianca was expected to work in the family kitchen preparing dishes like arrancini, amaretti and biscotti del Lagaccio to sell in the shop. I had time on my hands and joined the local library to learn all about local history. I didn't tell Bianca that I had done this. I wanted to surprise her. One Sunday, in March, with the temperature rising to just above freezing I heard on CBC radio that the ice on the Canal was considered unsafe so I decided to take Bianca on a historical tour. The sidewalks were slippy but we had become good at walking on icy surfaces. We had even become adept at looking up to avoid large melting icicles falling from eaves troughs on to our heads. We left my apartment in Kenwood Avenue, turned down Highland Avenue, crossed Byron and walked along the busy Richmond Road.

There we saw a building that was familiar to us but unfamiliar in Ottawa. It was built of stone and that was rare in the suburbs. Bianca, looked wide-eyed at the building and the little garden in front of it and said, 'that looks like a grander version of Rubers Hill Farmhouse'.

'It does, doesn't it? That's because it was built by an immigrant farmer who came from Cavers, one William Thomson'. I told Bianca that while she was slaving away in the deli kitchen I had been reading up on local history. I had discovered that William had made a fortune. He started out as a tenant farmer at Deanbrae on the Cavers Estate near Ruberslaw which we could see from my dad's farm at Rubers Hill. The Thomson family emigrated, sailing from Leith in 1817 on the sailing ship, *The Agincourt*. In those days the Canadian Government, much as it had started doing now, was trying to encourage immigrants to come to Canada. Settlers were granted 100 acres of Canadian wilderness. This was an attractive proposition because Thomson was only a tenant on a much smaller farm in Scotland. What Thomson did not bargain for was that wilderness meant wilderness. He had to clear near-impenetrable, dense old growth woodland to get shelter and create land for agricultural use. Thomson's 100 acres were here in what is now known as Ottawa. Thomson was a hard worker and cleared the land which serendipitously was in a very advantageous position next to the Ottawa River and opposite the Wrightsville trading post in

Quebec on the opposite side of the river. So in addition to farming wheat, oats and breeding sheep Thomson was involved in trading lumber and food on the Ottawa River all the way to the St Lawrence which was the main transport route in Canada at the time.

I had gleaned all this information from old copies of the *Bytown Gazette* I found in the library. Bianca was intrigued and amazed at the coincidence that we had ended up together in a foreign land that had such close links to home. Thomson became a very rich man owning large swathes of what is now Ottawa. He was a generous benefactor and built a fever hospital to nurse workers who were infected with malaria during the construction of the Rideau Canal. He used his wealth to build the house in front of us in 1831. Unlike the surrounding wooden buildings he built it in grey stone in the Georgian style popular with landed families in the Borders of Scotland. He named his new home Teviot Grove. After his death the name was changed to Maplelawn.

*　　*　　*

By the beginning of April most of the child evacuees had been returned to the UK and it looked as if my posting here was coming to an end. That was a bit of a worry because we had set a date in May for the wedding at St Andrews Church in Wellington Street. Just before Easter I was called into the High Commissioners office on the top floor. 'Singer, I have had a memo from the Foreign Office in London. Here, read it'.

Foreign Office London

April 1947

To: Office of High Commissioner, Canada

The euphoria after VE Day and VJ Day has proven to be short-lived. The costs of fighting the most expensive war in history has plunged the country into a series of economic crises and the economic assistance promised by President Truman is still just a promise. Cities are bomb-scarred, and housing shortages, which are exacerbated by returning troops, are critical. There are food and fuel shortages. Austerity and rationing food, fuel, furniture and clothing remain in place some two years after hostilities ended. Newly married couples are often forced to share with parents or to live in cold, inadequate homes.

We are forecasting a mass exodus of emigrants and many of them will be heading to Commonwealth countries like Canada. Indeed our latest estimates are that some 40,000 migrants from Great Britain went to Canada in 1946. I am also sure you will

be aware of a recent publicity stunt
carried out by George Drew, the Premier
of Ontario, when he flew over here to
hand out food parcels from the people of
Canada to hungry residents in Suffolk.
Furthermore, our intelligence is that the
Canadian Government is planning a major
campaign to encourage immigrants to come
to Canada.

What all this means is that it is a
matter of urgency that you prepare and
gear up for having to help an increase
in the number of British passport
holders coming to you for assistance.

'As you can see Singer there is going to be a rush on. It
is just as well that most of the child evacuees have been
sent home. You need to change the focus of your work.
I will give you an extra two executive officers to help.
I will inform the immigration people in the Canadian
Government and the next time I have lunch with the
editor of the *Ottawa Citizen* I will let him know that we
have this new service to help incoming Brits with
problems. It should certainly help people settle in. Go
to and get on with it'.

'Yes sir'. I walked slowly down the stairs. I had no
idea what to expect. Who would come for help? What
would they ask? I knew that most of the immigrants
came to Ontario but I had heard that an increasing

number of immigrants were settling in British Columbia and that was a three-day train journey away.

It wasn't long before I started to get answers to some of these questions. By the end of the week three people turned up seeking help. One couple found it so cold. The clothes they had brought with them weren't warm enough. Where was the best place to buy cheap warm clothing and were snow boots a good idea? That was easy to deal with. I said with Spring just round the corner to wait until the fall before buying new clothing. Their more immediate problem was that they would find it too hot and humid. I told them to buy a tin of Flit to keep the dreaded black fly at bay They went away happy. Another young man had a problem setting up a bank account because he had lost his passport and another older couple found that their sponsor had let them down and they needed help finding accommodation.

These kinds of minor problems, though they were far from minor for the landed immigrants concerned, became our bread and butter. There were more complex problems too which were more satisfying to deal with and more rewarding when you got a result. One interesting case involved a single woman who had worked in signals for the ministry of defence at Aldershot during the war. She came to Ottawa having been offered a specialist technical job in an unspecified government department. She came to see me after the Canadian Cabinet had introduced new security screening for immigrants. She had a Polish uncle who had immigrated to Montreal and that led her to be fired from her new job. Apparently her uncle was suspected of being a communist and was being investigated by the security services. I later found out that her uncle had fought for the allies as an officer in the Polish army but because Poland was now under the Soviet sphere of interest he was considered a potential enemy of the state. Sadly his war-time loyalties did not cut much ice with the Canadian security people. I was determined to help this lady. She was all alone in a foreign land. She did not have a job and would become destitute if she could not get her job back. She was a strong character and said, 'I will eventually find a job. In the meantime, if needs must, I can work the streets to keep body and soul together'. I liked her and had to help. I eventually persuaded the Canadians that they should employ her. I pointed out that she had rare specialist skills. But what clinched it was that I secured a reference from a senior official in the MoD in London who said that he vouched for her loyalty and that she was not a risk.

The area where there were most problems was that the Federal and Provincial governments did not always recognise foreign qualifications and in this case British qualifications were considered foreign. I was amazed to find that the authorities in Ontario required car mechanics to have a certificate of competence. I was approached by several time-served mechanics from England who were not offered a job because they did not have the correct qualifications. I said to go back to the garage boss, tell him you had so many years experience and that you would work without pay for three days and that he would find out that he didn't need to see a piece of paper to show him that you knew how to fix cars. There was such a shortage of car mechanics that this tactic worked every time. I had less success with nurses and physiotherapists who were trying to get work The Canadian authorities would not budge. A Miss Joan Martin came to see me. She had qualified and worked as a state registered nurse in London. No one would give her a hospital job. I remember her ranting, 'I was trained and worked in the hospital where Florence Nightingale was a nurse. Who are these people? How dare they not give me a job'? I told her she was fighting a losing battle and recommended that she train again to get a Canadian qualification. She went to the Wellesley School of Nursing in Toronto. She told me that this was 'ridiculous' but did admit, 'I actually learned a hell of a lot the second time around. You pick up things you didn't pick up the first time'.

My new job quickly became a big job. By the time my wedding came around we had helped over 100 people. I was promoted to the next grade. The extra income was very welcome but most importantly I had a settled job in Canada and would not be sent home to Scotland

Chapter 13   Bianca

1947 - Ottawa ON

For the first time in years I woke up every morning feeling great. The deli was going well, Hughie lived just down the road. I saw him every weekend and some evenings he would come over and help me in the kitchen. And, I had a wedding to look forward to. We decided that I would move into Hughie's apartment. It was quite big. It was on the second floor of a small block. There was a large kitchen, a living room, two bedrooms and one and a half bathrooms. There was also a small balcony and the outlook wasn't too bad. Kenwood Avenue was in an up and coming area; above all it was quiet and convenient for both of us to get to work. The British High Commission owned the house and rented it out to officials, most of whom only spent a couple of years in Ottawa before moving on to other countries or back to London. The furniture was a bit utilitarian, drab but functional. I would have to add my touches to make the place more colourful and homely.

When I wasn't working in the deli I was thinking about and planning the wedding. We felt the only place to get married was St Andrews Kirk. It was Church of Scotland and was the leading presbyterian church in Ottawa, if not the whole of Canada. St Andrews looks very Scottish. It is built in stone in the gothic revival style and is situated on the corner of Kent and

Wellington, surrounded on all sides by government buildings. It is huge and one of my worries was we would only have a few guests and we might look lost. The minister told us that, unlike the English Church that Hughie went to in Hawick, the pews were arranged in the tradition of the reformed churches and this meant that the congregation would feel part of a small cosy group. The guest list wasn't difficult. There was my family. Sadly it was too far and too expensive for Hughie's mum and dad to come. We both wrote to them to share our news and to let them know that we would send them photos and a piece of wedding cake each. Because Hughie and I spent all our time together we didn't really socialise so had few friends. Hughie had colleagues at work and the deli had some regular customers and suppliers who had to be invited. One of these was Mrs Ho Eng, a Chinese lady who was a regular in the deli and who was a seamstress, who was going to make my wedding dress. She said it was going to have hints of China, Canada, Italy and Scotland in it. I knew what she planned and couldn't wait to show it off. The reception was going to be in the Trattoria Romana in Preston Street. The restaurant had a lovely private room upstairs. There was also a small stage for a band. One of Hughie's colleagues was a fellow Scot from Glasgow. Duncan Cameron was his name. Away from work he was a fiddler and had formed a ceilidh band with some other Scottish ex pats in Kanata on the outskirts of town.

Towards the end of January I received an official looking envelope through the post. I opened it with some trepidation. The press had been full of stories about the new Canadian Citizenship laws and the deportation of Japanese immigrants to Japan. We still could not believe the Mounties' promise of Canadian citizenship and were concerned that we may have to give up the deli, be sent back to Scotland or Italy and of having to leave Hughie behind. In spite of all the other happy things happening in my life these fears were never far from my mind. The first thing I saw was the printed image of the crown followed by an invitation from His Excellency the Governor General, the Earl of Athlone, to attend a ceremony to honour my bravery at Rideau Hall at the end of February. That message was an enormous relief and I and the rest of the family had plenty of time to buy suitably smart clothing for the occasion - I still had my voucher from the Mounties.

Time rushed by and on the day in question a man in a chauffeur's uniform presented himself in the deli asking for Miss Bianca Carlucci. I was summoned from the flat upstairs. I had already donned my new frock and coat expecting a taxi to come and pick us up. The chauffeur, - I thought he was rather smart for a taxi driver - said, 'good morning Miss Carlucci would you like to follow me'. He took me outside and opened the door of a Rolls Royce limousine. Inside, sitting on sumptuous leather upholstery was a smiling Hughie looking magnificent in a morning suit. He smirked and said, 'I have borrowed this from the High Commissioner'.

We took the scenic route along Wellington Street past St Andrews Kirk, where we were going to get married, numerous government buildings and the Canadian Parliament. Once we got to the Chateau Laurier we took a sharp left and entered Sussex Drive. This was a long straight road running parallel to the Ottawa River. Sussex was flanked by more government buildings and several foreign embassies. Eventually we turned right into Rideau Hall.

The official residence of the Governor General was a large prepossessing stone building set at the end of a long drive in grounds covered in snow and surrounded by trees of all shapes and sizes. Just before we got to the Hall on the right there was a sight that one did not expect to see in Canada. There was a large flat open space and what looked like an old cricket pavilion. It reminded me of the Hawick and Wilton Cricket Club next to where I used to go to school. We were taken into one of the State Rooms. The Tent Room or La Salle de la Tente was a magnificent space. As its name suggested it looked like a tent with red and white striped wall paper rising into the ceiling which had an angled shape that made it look like a tent. Hanging from the apex of the tent roof were chandeliers that sparkled off the white and black marbled floor. I had never see the like before and it was a far cry from the tent we had to sleep in before they moved us into a hut at Camp B/70. The ceremony passed in a blur and it was not long before we were driving back up Sussex Drive where we turned right into Earnscliffe, the official residence of the British High Commissioner. For a moment I thought we had to return the Rolls Royce but we were greeted by a smartly dressed member of the commissioner corps. He said, 'welcome to Earnscliffe. The High Commissioner, Sir Alexander Clutterbuck is looking forward to seeing you in the drawing room'. Earnscliffe was relatively small and homely but it was still, after Rideau Hall, the largest house I had ever been in. The entrance hall with its mahogany staircase leading off was dominated by a large portrait of George VI. A door to the right led off into a dining room. There was a picture window at the end revealing a stunning view of the ice-covered Ottawa River. We were ushered through the door on the left. Standing in front of a large inglenook with a roaring fire was the imposing figure of Sir Alexander.

'Welcome my girl. We are all so proud of you. What you did was very brave and the information you were able to get out of these dastardly terrorists has saved many lives and no little embarrassment to the provincial government of New Brunswick and the federal government here in Ottawa'. Before I could say thank you for the loan of your car - because that was the first thing I could think of - the butler arrived at my side with a tray of champagne glasses. 'I raise a toast to the bravery of Miss Carlucci, a Scot born and bred, who found herself interred here through no fault of her own as an enemy alien. I must say that if this injustice had not been perpetrated then many people in this land of opportunity may have died. I give you Miss Carlucci'.

Chapter 14   Hughie

1948 - Ottawa ON & The Scottish Borders

We honeymooned in Gananoque, gateway to the legendary 1,000 islands on the St Lawrence River. It was very romantic and we stayed in the honeymoon suite of a lovely old inn which was surrounded on all sides by a covered verandah. The highlight for both of us was the honeymoon night. It was the night when Bianca probably became pregnant. By the fall Bianca was heavy in the belly and proudly showed off her new maternity clothes. We had endless discussions about what we should call the baby. If it was a girl Bianca favoured an Italian name like Lucia or Francesca. I preferred Scottish names like Morag or Margaret. We couldn't agree. It was the same with boys' names. What we did agree was that the baby should have three names. The first would be their Christian name. If it was a boy his second name would be Antonio after his maternal grandfather. If it was a girl her name would be Gina after Bianca's mother.

Our son was born in the maternity ward of the Ottawa Civic Hospital. Bianca's waters broke at three o'clock in the afternoon. Fortunately it hadn't snowed for three days and the temperature was a moderately balmy 28° F. The roads were clear and a taxi got us to the hospital without mishap. He was a lovely wee fellow. Everyone thought he looked like Winston

Churchill which I thought was a bit ironic given the origins of his grandfather. He was duly called Rory Antonio Singer and christened in St Andrews Kirk, with Mrs Eng as his godmother and Duncan Cameron his godfather. Under the new citizenship act Rory automatically became a Canadian citizen. I was a British subject and Bianca a landed immigrant - quite a complex international threesome, especially when you took the birthplaces of his grandparents into consideration.

Life with a baby in the house was different. Rory was a voracious eater and Bianca always seemed to be feeding him. He woke every night crying for his mother and after feeding cried some more from colic. We were so tired. How we managed to keep our tempers was a miracle. Gina said it would only be a phase. It didn't seem so at the time but Granny proved to know best. Rory grew into an adventurous toddler and was the life and soul at the mother and toddler group Bianca attended in Little Italy. It was great to have Gina as his grandmother as this gave Bianca and I some time for us to be on our own.

This time was precious as the High Commissioner's chief of staff, Alan Donald, told me that my tour of duty would be coming to an end and that I would be demobbed from the Air Force. What was especially problematic was that because of austerity in England the High Commission's budget had been reduced. It did not have the funding for an officer to head up a department to sort out British immigrants' problems. In any event the scale of the initial emigrant exodus had slowed. I had also set up a network of help using Anglican, Methodist and Presbyterian church volunteers right across Canada. My initiative was effectively doing me out of a job.

Talking to Mr Donald and Bianca we identified that there were plenty of jobs that I could do in Canada especially in Alberta and British Columbia. Bianca naturally was not keen to leave her parents but sadly there were fewer jobs locally from companies or organisations looking for my skills. I might be able to get work across the river in Quebec but sadly I could not speak French so that effectively ruled out that option. Mr Donald was pragmatic and helpful. We looked at the skills I had and what jobs might be a fit. We identified that my major skills were I was a qualified pilot and that I had considerable experience in administration in the emerging field of social work. I found out that, thanks to the war, there had been a growth of passenger air transport and that Trans-Canada Airlines, based nearby in Montreal, were looking for pilots. That sounded promising but when I looked into it the airline personnel officer told me that they preferred to recruit Canadian pilots. I pointed out that I had trained many of them to fly at Moncton. He was not impressed and said he wanted Canadian pilots and not English pilots. When I told him I wasn't English but Scottish he said, 'that's just the same'. So my future as an airline pilot never got off the ground. It was back to the drawing board.

Mr Donald was quite impressed with the way I had dealt with such a varied range of problems facing ex pat immigrants and the way I had set up a cross-Canada help network using the churches. He was convinced I should pursue a career in social and welfare work. Because of the war, the influence of the Beveridge Report and the ethos of the new Labour government in Britain, there was a distinct shortage of trained and experienced personnel in local authorities throughout England, Scotland and Wales. Mr Donald told me that he had a contact who was a big wheel in Roxburgh District Council and that's why our small family of three ended back living in the Borders of Scotland.

Chapter 15 Rory

1967 - Dundee

The train slowed to start the journey across the Tay Bridge. The river below was dark grey with white-topped waves scudding up stream. Looking out of the window, because the bridge curved round, I could see the engine with its smoke departing from the funnel in a near-horizontal manner. The engine slowed again as we pulled into Dundee Station. At the end of the platform there was a man in a janitor's uniform with a sign saying, 'New students go to the Caird Hall'. I struggled up the staircase with my heavy suitcase and followed a straggling procession of young men and women to a large stone building with Stalinesque grey columns.

Inside there was a bustling crowd of humanity nervously chatting to the people around them and wondering what was going to happen next. After about a quarter of an hour a middle aged-man wearing an academic gown with a dark blue hood appeared on the stage at the end of the cavernous hall. He tapped the lectern in front of him and in a very loud voice - he did not have a microphone - said, 'QUIET PLEASE. Welcome to Dundee as the first undergraduates in an independent University of Dundee. Until last year we were affiliated to St Andrews University and this year, 1967, we have become a fully independent new university with our own charter. You are therefore a very special and privileged group of students'. He then rabbited on about academic values and how those would make us the leaders of the future in whatever fields we chose to pursue. After what seemed like an interminable age he said 'I would now like to introduce you to Mrs Pritchard, the accommodation officer'.

Mrs Pritchard was a trendy-looking lady wearing a Mary Quant mini skirt, a bright red blouse and shiny black PVC beret. She was a far cry from the headmistress who ran the girls' section at school. She began, 'you are now adults and will be treated as such. There are no rules like you were used to at school. Actually I tell you a lie. Members of the opposite sex are not allowed to visit each others' study bedrooms in hall after ten o'clock at night. Anybody caught will be fined £5.00 and repeated offenders sent down'.

'You are here to learn, work hard and play hard. Our purpose at the new University of Dundee is to provide you with intellectual and social skills, as well as to advance learning through the development of critical thinking, the pursuit of knowledge and its dissemination. Your first three days will be spent in our orientation programme to help you get to know your way around. Later on I will tell you about your accommodation and where you will be living. Dundee is a small city in a great location near the sea and not far from the Highlands for those of you who like to explore. There is as wide a range of shops as you would expect to find in Edinburgh and Glasgow and you will be pleased to hear there are lots of pubs. Before you leave you will see that there are half a dozen tables with letters above them: A to D, E to H and so on each letter corresponding to your surname. There you will find a welcome pack which will give you all the information you need to to know as well as a map of the university buildings, departments and facilities. Be sure to check out where the Students Union Building is. The Union contains: bars, a canteen, a shop, a hall and lots of other facilities. As students you are automatically a member of the Union and I recommend you go along there tomorrow when various societies and groups will be setting out their wares and trying to encourage your participation. Your welcome pack also contains information about the Library which is running familiarisation tours during your first week here. I strongly recommend you attend one of these. Also in your pack are details of your accommodation. Sadly we do not have a large enough number of study bedrooms to house you all in the halls of residence. This means about half of you will be lodged in digs which are located throughout the city. Most digs are within walking distance of the main lecture theatre block. The digs are owned and operated by private landlords but vetted by the university. At least two students of the same sex will share each of the digs. I have visited a number of them and they are not bad. Next year those of you who have lived in digs will have a preferential option of moving into hall. Students in hall and in digs will not have to pay rent. That money will automatically be taken out of your grant cheque received by the university. All you will have to pay for is your food, books, clothing, subs for societies, sundry charges like entrance fees to the swimming pool and of course for booze and fags'. For her last remark she got a big laugh. Everything was strange and a bit forbidding but Mrs Pritchard gave me a feeling that I was going to enjoy myself.

I made my way over to the table signed S to Z looking through the pile of welcome folders laid out in alphabetical order. I found mine just as another hand grabbed the one marked Sinclair M. 'Hi I'm Mark Sinclair. Who are you? I answered, 'Rory Singer from Hawick studying history'. He responded, 'I'm doing history too and I'm from Linlithgow. Given that our folders are next to each other I wonder if we'll be billeted nearby'? I pulled the rubber band off my folder and read that I would be in digs at 18 Arthurstone Terrace, sharing with a student called Mark Sinclair.

My first impressions of Mark had been positive. He was about four inches taller than me and quite broad. He had the look of a second row forward but, coming from Linlithgow, I doubt he played rugby. He gave me a broad grin, shook my hand and said, 'so we have been billeted together. I hope you smoke and drink like me'. I grinned back and said, I like the odd pint but I don't smoke and provided you don't smoke in bed we should get along' - I noticed in the pack that there were two single beds in the bedroom.

'Where is Arthurstone Terrace'?

'I haven't a clue. There's a map pinned up on the wall over there'. We pushed our way through the crowd of fellow students.' It looks quite a long way from here. Probably within walking distance though not with heavy suitcases. Let's get a tram'. I had noticed on the walk over from the station that Dundee had a fleet of bright green double decker trams. We made our way out of the Caird Hall and caught a tram in the Nethergate. Fortunately the map had shown the number of the tram we would need to catch to the digs. I had never been to Dundee before. Everything was strange and new - actually it was old. Everything was Victorian and covered in a film of smelly jute dust. Normally I would have travelled on the upper deck but with such heavy cases we both settled for downstairs with the old folks in the non smoking section where the signs read 'No Smoking, No Spitting'. I spent the short journey looking out of the window. Two things struck me. They were that Dundee was a hilly place and one with Royalist leanings. At the bottom of a steep hill was King Street. We then went up Princess Street, before crossing Victoria Road into Albert Street after which the clippie rang the bell and yelled out in a strong Dundee accent, 'Athurstane Terrace'.

18 Arthurstone Terrace was a three storey sandstone tenement next to the British Legion Club. We were on the top floor up three flights of grubby stone steps and graffiti strewn walls. It was a hard slog going up and when we found the key under the mat Mark said, 'I noticed a coal house for each set of digs in the wee garden at the back. We'll have to organise a rota for carrying up the coal and taking the ashes down each morning'.

There were two sets of digs on the top floor and both had solid brown varnished front doors with a brass letterbox. The digs were clean but a little on the small side. The furniture was obviously second-hand utility furniture built after the war. At least the desks and three book shelves above were new. There were two rooms off a tiny entrance hall which had a built in cupboard containing a Ewebank carpet sweeper and hooks for our coats. At the front was a bedroom with twin beds squeezed next to each other - I hoped Mark didn't snore. At the back the main room contained the desks, a couple of chairs and a table in front of a large black range and fireplace. There was a tiny scullery with a sink, a gas cooker and space for only one person. The small room next to the bedroom contained a cracked WC, a wash hand basin and a towel rail coming off the wall. The views at the front and back could not be more different. At the front was the Broadway Cinema. It had a large blue and red neon sign that alternated between 'Broadway' and 'Cinema'. It took several weeks to get used to the light shining through the threadbare curtains. The view from the back was magnificent. In front of the large window was a coal bunker with a light brown varnished top which we could sit on and stare over the rooftops and over the Firth of Tay to Newport and Tayport in Fife. We also used the bunker to stand on when we needed to peg out our washing on the pulley which was attached from the wall next to the window to a large pole at the end of the garden where there was also a wash house with a copper boiler, aluminium washboard and wooden mangle.

After unpacking and familiarising ourselves with the digs we went on a hunt for a grocer's shop.

We found a high class grocers nearby in Dura Street. We bought a loaf of bread, some beans, a tin of soup, Camp Coffee, a couple of bottles of Irn-Bru and some stuff for breakfast. Mr Spence, the grocer, was a nice man and said he could arrange to have rolls delivered to the digs each morning. We ordered two morning rolls and two butteries, a delicious east coast speciality. He could also arrange milk deliveries and did we want one pint or two. We plumped for one to begin with. Neither of us had ever had to organise or prepare meals before so this was a voyage of discovery.

We had a leisurely breakfast and around half ten we made our way to the Union building. We walked and found a couple of short cuts. The Union was packed out. There were tables and stalls round the walls and two rows in the middle of the floor. The choice of activities and pursuits was staggering. I noticed rugby next to football. In sport there was also gymnastics, archery, cricket, judo, fencing and mountaineering as well as others. Beyond sport there was philately, chess, Christianity and Judaism, country dancing, poetry, music etc., etc. The largest stalls were political. There were the Young Socialists, Young Conservatives, communists, anarchists and Scottish nationalists. Mark and I cruised round the stalls trying to take it all in and after half an hour went off for a coffee and a Forfar bridie. We sat down and I said, 'that was some choice. There will never be enough time in the day to do a fraction of what was on offer'. Mark nodded, scratched his chin and said, 'did you notice there were a lot more blokes than crumpet'? 'No', I replied, 'but come to think of it we outnumbered the girls by at least four to one'. I paused, 'that's not a good outlook.' Mark agreed and said, 'I noticed a lot of women at the Young Conservatives' stall and there were a couple of crackers on the desk especially the brunette. Let's away and join the YCs'. 'No way,' I exclaimed. I am not a Tory. Dad is a social worker and a Liberal activist. He actively campaigned for David Steel who is currently working on a private member's bill to legalise abortion. I would be *persona non grata* if I joined the Tories.' Mark countered, 'come on. If your father is a genuine liberal he would respect your choice'. 'I'm not sure'. Mark persisted, 'at least let's go and have a look. The two on the desk were real crackers. I baggsy the brunette. You can have the blonde; she has a lovely pair'.

We set off back to the hall and the two girls were still on the desk and he was right about the blonde's attributes. Mark was a great chat up merchant and was easily persuaded to sign up for YC membership. I joined too. The girls were very friendly and accepted our invitation to go to the bar for a drink provided they could go Dutch. We both had pints and they had Babychams followed by a half of lemonade shandy each. I have never taken so long to drink a pint. We sat in the bar until after it closed at three o'clock. The four of us talked and talked and during our conversation we learned all about each other, in the process discovering some amazing coincidences. Once we had taken our drinks back to the red plastic couchette the blonde said, 'let's tell each other about ourselves'. She looked at me and said, 'you start'. I told the others, my name, that

I had been born in Canada, lived in the Borders, that my dad was a social worker and I was studying history and had digs in Arthurstone Terrace. At this the blonde interrupted, 'we live in Arthurstone Terrace too' - it transpired that their digs were next to ours on the top floor of number 18. 'My name is Kathleen Solomon. I also come from the Borders. My dad runs a garage and car dealership. I study history too, with philosophy as a subsidiary subject'. She looked at me closely. I blushed ever so slightly but it felt as if my cheeks were on fire before asking, 'where did you go to school'. 'I went to Hawick High School'. She said, 'I thought I recognised you. You were in the year above me and were a spotty youth who was the star of the rugby team. I am pleased to tell you that your complexion has improved'. I had no recollection of her at all. We didn't notice girls in the year below. I did remember her dad's garage though at the end of the High Street.

Kathleen drew breath and pointed to Mark and said, 'your turn'. I had only met Mark the day before and in spite of sharing the same bedroom the night before I was all ears to find out more. It turned out that he was an only child and that his dad spent as much time on social security as in picking up jobs as a plumber's mate. He was the first in his family to go to university, just as I was. Last but not least was the brunette. Like Kathleen she was very pretty. Lorna Smyth also had an English accent having lived in Cheshire all her life with her mother and father, who was a solicitor, a member of the Conservative Party and chairman of the general purposes committee on Manchester

City Council. Lorna was studying for a degree in politics, economics and history. At half past three we got thrown out of the bar and we agreed to meet in our digs later that night where we shared a convivial supper of a reconstituted Vesta chow mein and a Fray Bentos pie.

The following day after the induction tour of the library we all trooped into lecture theatre number four. There were about fifty students sitting in rows tiered above the lecturer. The four of us sat together at the back. The first person to appear at the lectern was the dean. He looked ancient with flowing grey hair, a gown covered in cigarette ash over a rather worn tweed jacket. He was wearing what I was later told was a Balliol College tie. He welcomed us to the history faculty, explaining that the course consisted of lectures, seminars in tutorial groups, reading - lots of reading - and investigating primary sources, whatever these were. We were all told that our seminar groups were led by our tutorial supervisor to whom we would have to submit two essays a month. Because the university did not know the students before they arrived tutor group membership was determined by names in alphabetical order. That meant that, serendipitously, the four of us would all be in the same seminar group with a Dr Tom Drake our supervisor. The dean said that a feature of our course was that, periodically, leading academics from other universities would address us now and again. He concluded his remarks saying, 'today I have the great pleasure to welcome Dr T C Smout from Edinburgh University to the podium'.

I had heard of Chris Smout and knew he was a rising star. He had recently published *Scottish Trade on the Eve of Union, 1660–1707* which received critical acclaim. He was a tall bespectacled young man going bald on top but with bushy hair over his ears at the back of his head. You could tell from his demeanour that he was passionate and enthusiastic. When he opened his mouth I was surprised to hear that he was English. Until now I thought all Scottish historians would have been Scottish. Dr Smout was inspirational. He said that in recent years there had been a revolution in the way history was taught. In the old days it was all about Kings, Queens, Generals and Bishops, what he called history from above. Today the emphasis had changed to history from below looking at timeline trajectories from the point of view of the masses, the labourers, the factory workers and the unemployed. He said that one of the greatest changes was the growing interest in the role of women. He suggested that perhaps this should be called herstory - this drew a laugh from Kathleen and Lorna. He closed by inviting us to challenge and question and to take lessons from developments in historiography led by Marxist historians like E P Thompson and R H Tawney. How that suggestion went down with our new YC friends remained to be seen. After the lecture we went our separate ways.

*   *   *

About 7 o'clock there was a knock on the door. It was Kathleen who announced, 'it transpires that Lorna is a bit of a cook and she has made a curry. There is enough to feed an army and we have a bottle of Warninks Advocaat and some Blue Nun. You guys are welcome to join us'. Mark and I had planned to go to the chippy and this sounded a much better idea. 'Give us five minutes and we will go round to the Off Licence to get a few beers'. I had never drunk wine or advocaat, what ever that was, before and thought that this would be a wise move. It also gave us time to top up on the aftershave and deodorant.

The conversation over supper was very intellectual. We had all enjoyed Dr Smout's lecture and were excited about looking at history in a new and much more adult way. At school it was just a series of dates 1314, 1603, 1707, 1745, 1815 and on and on and on. I discovered I liked wine and both bottles were consumed with a consequent effect of raising the decibel level. When Lorna cleared the plates and put them in the sink, Kathleen brought out a pack of cards and poured out four shots of white sticky advocaat. I looked at it with suspicion. It was sweet and sickly, looking a bit like a rich custard. It tasted of vanilla, sugar and brandy and my goodness it packed a kick. We all downed our shots in one. Kathleen topped up our glasses and said, 'lets play pontoon and because we are all poor students we will play for matches and not for money. I'll give you all seven matches each and the first person to lose them all has to do a forfeit which I suggest is carrying up the coal buckets for both our digs for a week. The winner of each hand, the first to get to twenty one, will receive a match from the other three and so pots will go up and down until one of us has no matches left'. While Kathleen doled out the matches Mark put some coal on the fire and Lorna shuffled and dealt out the cards. I won the first hand and my pot of matches went up to ten. I also won the second hand with my cut going up to thirteen, eight ahead of each of the others. I thought I was safe from coal bucket duty. After another hand which I lost Lorna said, 'what about another shot'? After three more hands we had another shot and another after three more hands. The lead in matches was going backwards and forwards and it looked like no one was ever going to be required to hump the coal up three flights of stairs. Kathleen poured another shot and said, 'let's make the game a bit more exciting. Instead of the losers having to give up matches, in my game the losers will have to take off an item of clothing'. By that stage of the evening all of us had lost all vestiges of our Presbyterian upbringings and readily agreed to the new game.

The new game followed the pattern of the first with me winning the first two hands. After the first Mark took off his shoes, a scruffy pair of winkle pickers. After the second hand Mark took off his socks and the girls their tights. I was feeling somewhat smug. I lost the next five games in a row and was in a greater state of undress than the others. After taking my jumper off leaving only my shirt, jeans and Y-Fronts I suggested another drink. The advocaat was finished so we opened a couple of bottles of beer and shared that around. A few hands later the girls were down to their bras and pants and we only had our Y-Fronts on. At this stage my nervousness was trumping my state of excitement. It was essential that either Mark or I won the next hand. To my great relief Mark was the first one to call pontoon. The girls checked his hand and with some reluctance took off their bras. I had never seen girls breasts before. They were magnificent. While I was looking at the difference in sizes the black slate clock on the mantlepiece struck twelve. The witching hour was upon us. Lorna shuffled and Mark dealt the cards. This was the slowest hand we played and it looked as if no one was going to go bust as we all strove to get to twenty one. Eventually Kathleen called pontoon. There was a prolonged silence. The atmosphere was tense, with a mixture of apprehension and excitement. Kathleen broke the silence and said, 'when I was at primary school we used to play doctors and nurses. Rory and Mark I see you both have large lumps in your underpants. I think that Lorna and I had better check that you are ok'. At that the girls moved towards us. Kathleen said, 'we are going to give your lumps a gentle squeeze. The first person to twitch will have to carry the coal up for a week'. As her fingers touched me through the fabric the rag rug in front of the fire suddenly became the setting of my first orgy. There were eight legs, eight arms, eight hands, four breasts and four throbbing loins writhing in asymmetric unison.

Chapter 16   Kathleen

1967-8 - Dundee

After that first eventful night in Uni Rory and I became soulmates. We saw each other every day and because we both lived in Hawick we even saw each other during vacations. Our relationship grew to be very strong, not just physically and emotionally but intellectually and politically as well. During our first year we had a tremendous row with the university authorities and were even summoned to appear before a senate committee.

It all began when we challenged and picketed our tutor. Dr Tom Drake was one of the new breed of Marxist historians mentioned by Dr Smout in our inaugural lecture. Tom, who insisted we use his first name unlike all the other academics who we had to call Dr or Professor was a charismatic, likeable character but he was also a Marmite character. He told us to question, question and question the historiography but became very defensive and sometimes aggressive when we questioned his views. Our tutor was young, late twenties, and always wore jeans and a black polo neck. He had a stubby beard and could have benefited from spending some of his salary on Brut deodorant.

Our seminars were always interesting. Tom showed us how to find and assemble the facts before conducting a critical analysis to develop hypotheses which we should seek to disprove to establish our initial hypothesis' validity. He was very definitely of the history from below school and this did mean we were taken to interesting topics and themes that were not part of the history we had been taught at school. My problem with Tom was that he was profoundly anti-English and that affected me personally. He was also very prejudiced, arguing that only a Marxist interpretation was a valid one. His lectures and seminars where full of concepts like the dialectic, the proletariat and the bourgeoisie. His position was evident from our first topic which was the Act of Settlement in 1707. According to him Scotland was scunnered by their voracious neighbour to the south, by wealthy English aristocrats bribing Scottish members of parliament, who were largely from the Scottish aristocracy or bourgeoisie. Robbie Burns described these Scots as fools who sold out for parcels of gold. To complete Tom's Marxist determinism we were informed that the mob or proletariat frequently rioted in opposition to the treaty in the streets of Edinburgh, and that they were put down and ignored. At the time I didn't have the knowledge or the historical skills to argue with this interpretation but both Lorna and I felt distinctly uncomfortable with Tom's open and blatant hatred of the English.

Over the next few weeks we met up with the boys in each others digs to share a meal. The antics of our first night were not repeated. We were altogether more civilised, discussing and debating the lecture and seminar topics. We also talked about politics, the goings on in *Coronation Street* and listened to records - our favourites were the Beach Boys, the Four Tops, the

Spencer Davis Group and Dusty Springfield. We didn't play pontoon again and played bridge instead. We didn't get drunk although we drank and got a little merry on occasion. Unlike some other members of our seminar group none of us experimented with LSD which was readily available in Dundee. There was one occasion when we did get a bit silly but that never rivalled the first night. That was when we, along with countless other students, crammed into the television room in the Union building. We had come to watch Celtic, the first British team to appear in a European cup final, play the Italian team, Internazionale, in Lisbon, Portugal. Rory was wearing a green and white T shirt. I had on my new and very bright ancient Buchanan mini kilt. Rory said it was a pelmet and not a mini skirt. Mark, who certainly was not a Celtic supporter, was wearing a blue shirt. Traditional enmities had been set aside for the occasion. When the final whistle went the room erupted and Rory whispered or rather shouted in my ear. He said he wanted to wear my mini kilt for the rest of the evening. In a state of euphoria I agreed and took it off. He dropped his trousers and donned my mini kilt. It was a wee bit tight on him. I on the other hand wallowed in his trousers. True to his word Rory wore my mini kilt for the rest of the evening of celebrations and he was even offered a free drink by the barman in the Salty Dog.

*   *   *

It was the way that Tom dealt with the clearances that brought matters to a head. His fundamental thesis was that English aristocrats, the bourgeoisie, and the capitalist system engaged in an ethnic purge of Highland crofters, the proletariat, and expelled them to Canada. Once there, with gifts of land, the crofters became members of the bourgeoisie. In turn they forced the local indigenous tribes off their lands in the same way as they were cleared off theirs and replaced with sheep. Tom also appeared to contradict himself by referring to the cleared crofters as down-trodden refugees who suddenly became rapacious capitalists once they landed in Pictou, Pugwash or Prince Edward Island.

We all had to write essays on the subject. Lorna, in particular, was incensed at Tom's anti-English bias. She argued very strongly that, in her opinion, the majority of the landlords who cleared crofters off their estates were Scottish and that Tom's characterisation of this group as Anglos who went to English public schools and who owned large houses in London did not accord with the facts. A large red line and the word RUBBISH was written next to that argument in Lorna's essay. Tom dwelt on one group who were cleared and that was the 10,000 crofters who were violently removed from the Duke of Sutherland's estate in the north east Highlands. The Duke had been born in England. He went to Westminster School and Christ Church College, Oxford. He was an MP in Staffordshire before he married into the Sutherland family. Tom posited that this English-born duke was typical of most estate owners clearing their lands of human inhabitants. Lorna argued that the evidence contradicted this conclusion pointing out that Sutherland's factor, Patrick

Sellar, who did the dirty work, had been born along the coast in Moray and was a Scottish lawyer to boot. Tom's red scrawl said, 'to boot was not academic language'. The final straw was the mark: 15 out of 100.

The day that our essays were handed back was the day when Enoch Powell was the guest speaker at one of the YC monthly soirées. It was a bit of a coup for the YCs to get such a high profile speaker. In recent weeks he was rarely out of the news having given his infamous Rivers of Blood speech at a meeting in Birmingham during the middle of our Easter vacation. When we were planning future meetings last October we wanted Powell to talk about his spell as Minister of Health. That had been quite a controversial period when he raised prescription charges and had been instrumental in creating new district hospitals with smaller wards as well as tearing down many Victorian lunatic asylums to be replaced with care in the community. Our initial plans for him to talk about health policy were thrown out of the window with the furore he created when he divided the nation with a single speech that claimed Britain itself was a divided nation and that Britain must be mad - "literally mad"- to allow an annual influx of 50,000 foreign families. He said this was like piling up the nation's funeral pyre. The left and many newspapers claimed that he was an irresponsible evil racist.

A week before he was due in Dundee we discovered just how incendiary his visit could be. I was the secretary of the YCs at the time and I had a message from a Chief Superintendent Morris. He invited me and a couple of other committee members to a meeting at the police station, not far away from the university in West Bell Street. At that meeting we were told that the police had intelligence that a group of young socialists, anarchists and some trade unions had planned a massive demonstration and that the police were concerned that there would be violent disturbances. To outflank the demonstrators Chief Superintendent Morris suggested that we move the meeting to the large seminar room at Ninewells Hospital, a couple of miles from the university, and that we should inform members of the YCs that attendance would be restricted to members only and that they should keep the change of venue secret.

The day came and we were already more fired up than usual with all four of us incurring more of Tom's red pen than usual because we had all challenged Tom's thesis about the English being responsible for the clearances and the way in which proletariat crofters morphed into bourgeois land owners clearing the indigenous tribes of Canada off their ancestral lands. Our new venue at Ninewells was packed to the rafters and we lost some of the usual intimate atmosphere, but the way Powell spoke and engaged in discussion was mesmerising. He fired us up and was indirectly responsible for us starting our anti-Drake campaign.

I must admit with my boyfriend's family containing German and Italian ancestry I was a little uncomfortable about some of Powell's conclusions. His main proposition that integration of immigrants was difficult had some merit. What concerned me was some of his inflammatory language. He argued that the Labour government's recent

Race Relations Act was like throwing a match on to gunpowder. What I particularly objected to was when he referred to immigrants' children as wide-grinning piccaninnies.

But he was very persuasive, as one might expect from someone who was also a professor of Greek. He was intellectually stimulating and gave us food for thought as we were all still fuming about Tom's responses to our essays. At the end of his talk, also striking for its delivery in a strong black country accent, Powell asked if there were any questions.

Rory was second up and openly said that he was distressed at being made to accept an uncorroborated Marxist interpretation of history and how his tutor conflated the concepts of refugees, emigrants and immigrants. He explained how Tom had posited that exploited crofters, violently ejected from their homes, were members of the proletariat and that when they were given land in Canada they were considered to be capitalist immigrants. Rory asked if Powell thought there were any lessons that could be applied from the present situation in Britain. Powell answered that, on the whole, Marxist interpretations of history were deeply flawed and that that these ideas should be challenged. A rigorous debate followed in which Rory and Powell challenged and rebutted each other. Powell ended by conceding that the definition of who was an immigrant was not always easy to determine. He admitted that British men were finding themselves strangers in their own country and that the presence of so many coloured immigrants was making it difficult for their wives to find beds in maternity hospitals. He accepted, though, that many of the doctors and nurses were also coloured and that they were not immigrants, they were citizens of a Commonwealth country who had come here for education or to serve the mother country. He was emphatic when he said that this meant they were not, and never had been, immigrants.

The meeting eventually came to a close. Normally we took visiting speakers for a drink and a bite to eat. Powell, though, said that he had to get the sleeper back to London. In the taxi to the station Powell told Rory that he had been impressed with the effectiveness of his arguments and that if he wanted a career in politics when he graduated to get in touch. He gave him his card.

*   *   *

Not long before Powell's visit the newspapers were full of stories about the student protest movement, especially the sit-ins in Paris. That gave us an idea. The following evening, still fuming at Tom's reaction to our essays, after our third beer Mark said, 'what about a sit-in in Tom's office. 'Yeah'. 'Yeah'. 'Yeah'. We all chanted in unison. 'She loves you, And you know that can't be bad' sang Rory. We all fell about laughing.

When sanity had been restored I said, 'that's not a bad idea. That ought to make him sit up and listen. How are we going do it and what are we going to ask for'? The room filled up with furrowed brows. I continued, 'it shouldn't be too difficult. His office is on the second floor overlooking a flat roof below. All we need is a ladder to climb up and break in. And if, like the students at the Sorbonne, it is a long sit-in, we will be able to get in and out to get supplies without having to run the gamut of the authorities and janitors, who are bound to be outside the locked door in the corridor'.

'That sounds like a plan. Simple, practical and feasible', said Lorna. None of us had done any breaking or entering before and wondered how to get through a window that was bound to be snibbed shut. 'I know', said Lorna, 'And this is deliciously ironical. Because I am English I bank with Barclays Bank and they have just issued me with one of these new Barclaycards. We can use this to slide between the sash, shift the snib and open the window'. We spent the rest of the evening gathering food, drink and other bits and pieces together. At half past six we went to the janitor's room, which was never locked, and took out one of his ladders. We went to the front of the building and once we were all on the flat roof we pulled up the ladder so we could come and go without detection. We found the Barclaycard really was our flexible friend and we were in as easy as that.

Tom had a decent sized office. The wall behind his desk was given over to shelves full of books written by authors like Marx, Engels, Fanon, Gramsci, Ho Chi Min, Lenin, Sartre, Tawney, Trotsky and E P Thompson amongst others. In the middle of his desk, next to an Imperial typewriter, was a copy of *The Little Red Book* by Chairman Mao. From the window there was a stunning view over the river with the Tay Bridge right in the middle. The tide was out revealing the sandbank where we rowed out to play a football match during rag week. This morning we could see three basking seals which we considered a good omen.

Once we were settled in and had made sure that the door was locked we put the back of a chair under the handle to make sure no one could get in. We made ourselves comfortable and had some breakfast. We shared a tin of Trout Hall grapefruit and had a roll each we picked up from the bakers on the way here. I said,'the first thing we need to do is to tell the world why we are here and to set out our demands'. Everyone agreed and Lorna said we need to start by pinning a sign on the outside of the door. Mark agreed and Rory found some blank sheets of paper in the top left hand drawer of the desk along with a box of red marker pens and some sellotape. 'What shall we put'? 'I know', said Lorna and scrawled in large capital letters

SIT-IN IN PROGRESS

KEEP OUT

DRAKE MUST GO

PUT AN END TO BIAS AND PREJUDICE

'That's perfect' I said. We all signed it, opened the door and fixed it to the outside. It was still early in the morning and there was no one about. Lorna, who had quietly assumed a leadership role, announced that we must write and issue a press release and telephone it through to the editor of the *Courier* before they cut Tom's phone off.

We had discussed our demands and what we wanted to achieve until the wee small hours. There was general agreement that we wanted our essays to be marked and regraded by an historian from another university, someone like Dr Smout. We could not agree what we wanted to happen to Tom or if we wanted to transfer to another of the lecturers' seminar groups. Lorna was the most strident and wanted Tom to be sacked. While the rest of us understood and shared her anger we were realistic enough to realise because of academic freedom it was virtually impossible to fire a sitting academic. We eventually agreed that we should ask that the university authorities should reprimand him and send him on some training course that would make him realise the error of his ways.

Writing out our statement of demands was relatively easy and given that I had attended a secretarial course before I came to uni I typed out the statement on Tom's typewriter, It took me about twenty minutes with liberal use of Tippex. I checked it and called the editor of the *Courier*. 'Good morning, my name is Kathleen Solomon I represent a group of students conducting a protest sit-in in the office of Dr Tom Drake at the University of Dundee. We object in the strongest possible terms to his racist anti-Englishness and his trenchant Marxist views about which he rejects all rational criticism and questioning. As such he is not fit to hold an academic position at the new University of Dundee. As a result of his bias and prejudice our essays on the highland clearances have been unfairly marked down. We demand that our essays are marked and re-graded by an historian from another university. Furthermore we demand that Dr Drake is reprimanded by the Vice Chancellor and that he is fined the equivalent of a month's salary'. 'Miss what's your name again'? responded the editor. I hung up. I did not want to engage in a dialogue at this early stage. I knew that the editor would telephone the university authorities for a comment which meant that our sit-in would be noticed and that something would have to be done about it.

Sure enough after ten minutes we heard a key being placed in the keyhole followed by a banging on the door. Fortunately our make-shift barricade held firm. A voice called out, 'we know you are in there. Open up so we can talk.' Rory replied, 'there will be no talking until you give in to our demands. We are here for the long haul. We have enough food for days'. He added rather cheekily, 'we have also brought a pail with us and as students of history we are all aware of how piss and crap were thrown out of windows in medieval times - *gardez l'eau*.' We all laughed and we could hear the person in the corridor walk away to the far end.

'First round to us then' said Lorna. 'We'll just have to sit tight and see what happens next.' Nothing happened for the rest of the morning. The university authorities were either trying to work out their response or were deliberately ignoring us hoping that we would give up. About three o'clock we heard footsteps in the corridor and a voice, obviously amplified by a loud hailer said, 'I am Professor Robinson from the vice-chancellor's office. We would like to talk to you. We have been worried about some of Dr Drake's attitudes for some time.' Rory whispered, 'I think it's a trick to get us to give up'. Mark shouted in a loud voice, 'we are staying put until you give in to our two demands. They are that our essays are independently marked and regraded and that Dr Drake is either fined a month's salary or sent on a training course to change his attitudes.'

'That's what we want to talk about' responded Professor Robinson, 'come out'.

'We'll come out when you agree to our demands.'

'Let's talk first'.

'No. You have to agree to our demands first'.

This stalemate went on for about half an hour and Professor Robinson said he was going away to talk to the vice chancellor, adding that he would be back. We could hear him walk down the corridor and open and close the door at the end. He did not come back until the following morning clearly hoping that we would be tired, hungry and fed up. He did not understand our anger or our determination to stay put until we got what we wanted. The professor had not come back with anything new to say and there was a repetition of the disagreement we had yesterday. That ended when he said that he needed to talk to the vice chancellor again. For a second time he did not come back until the following day, the third day of the sit-in. Unknown to us the story of the sit-in made the front-page of the *Courier* and it was picked up by the national newspapers and STV. On the third morning Professor Robinson was much more conciliatory. He said that if we came out he would guarantee that our essays would be marked and regraded by a history lecturer from another Scottish University and that the university authorities in Glasgow and St Andrews had agreed to do this. The professor said that he could not agree to our demands that Dr Drake be reprimanded but that he could make arrangements for us to present our case and grievances to the appropriate senate subcommittee. We all whooped and shrieked. We had won and the sit-in ended.

Chapter 17   Kathleen

1972 - London

The rest of our days at university passed uneventfully. We all got good degrees and interesting graduate trainee jobs in London. Rory and I talked about getting married but my mother and father would not grant me permission to marry a gentile. Rory was adamant that he was not going to be circumcised so we decided to live together, much to the disapproval of both sets of parents. We shared a house with four junior doctors practicing in St Thomas' Hospital which was close to our Victorian terraced house in de Laune Street. We had two rooms in the basement and shared a kitchen with the doctors. They were a great bunch of guys and we had some smashing parties. There was only one area of friction and that was the state of the kitchen. They never washed their dishes or cleared up. We regularly used to moan that they were growing penicillin in the sink to give to their patients.

Our first house together was a bit of a dump. We had rented it furnished and the furniture left a lot to be desired. We were so envious when we looked through the windows of shops like Habitat and Heals. The bed though was at least comfortable. The big problem was that our basement bedroom was directly above the Northern Line. Our proximity to the London Underground led us to experience more vibrations than our normal nocturnal activity. The bedroom itself was fairly small and one side of the bed abutted a rather damp outside wall. The best thing about de Laune Street was its location. It was about half an hour from both our offices. I had managed to get a job as a graduate trainee in the transportation department of the Greater London Council. My office which I shared with fifteen others was in an inside courtyard of County Hall and we didn't benefit from the wonderful views at the front looking over the Thames to the Houses of Parliament and New Scotland Yard. There were two rows of desks facing each other with the manager, Mr Frank Turner, sitting at the end. Sitting opposite me was a leery lech, Jeremy James. All too often he would take his shoes off, and because there wasn't a modesty board he would slide his foot up the inside of my leg. He also had the unfortunate habit of coming over my side of the desk, putting his hand round my shoulder and trying to look down my front. I tried complaining to Mr Turner. He said he couldn't do anything about it and said I had to accept it as I was a woman. One day when Jeremy was rubbing my leg I slid down in my chair and gave him an almighty kick where it hurt. I was never troubled again.

My work was very interesting but what I found hard to believe was how inefficient and bureaucratic working for local government could be. My main job was to draft answers to questions from members of the public and central government departments. I once had to draft a letter on behalf of the Queen who had been sent a letter by one of her subjects asking for information about the Council's road building plans. When I started work at the GLC there was a lot of public interest and anxiety about the council's plans to build a network of motorways around and within London There was the outer orbital Ringway 3, then Ringway 2 through the suburbs to Ringway 1 round the centre. Most of the concern was about planning blight and the demolition of houses required for roadbuilding. People were understandably worried if their house was going to be knocked down. Not surprisingly there was a good deal of protest and we often had to walk through jostling groups of demonstrators outside County Hall. The first part of my job was the really interesting part; then I was faced with enormous frustration. On receipt of a letter I would have to go to the relevant technical, planning or legal department to get information to draft an answer on behalf of the Director of Transportation. I would handwrite my draft and send it to the typing pool. The typed version would come back to me a few days later and I would put it in Mr Turner's in box where it usually sat for a couple of days. Mr Turner would check it and send corrections back to me. Sometimes these were trivial and sometimes not. The amended letter would go back to the typing pool for retyping and come back to me corrected. I would then place the new version in Mr Turner's boss' in box. He usually took days to approve it and more often than not he made further changes. The process went round again until the letter eventually arrived on the director's desk for signature.

One day I got a handwritten letter on blue Basildon Bond writing paper from an old age pensioner, a Mrs Ethel Morrison. She explained that she was a war widow who had lived in her house since 1938 when she got married. She had read in the *Evening Standard* that her house was going to be demolished for the Ringway. I did my research as usual and in doing so established she lived some 250 yards away from the planned route and her house was safe. I don't know why but this letter touched me and I was furious knowing that the system I operated under would mean that it was weeks before she would get the good news. When I finished my handwritten draft I added a P.S. apologising for taking so long saying the typing pool in the Council was somewhat slow and inefficient. Well if ever there was a volcanic eruption in County Hall that was it. When the typist saw my draft she reported if to her supervisor who reported it to her boss, then to his boss all the way up to the Director of Supplies who contacted the Director of Transportation and the message speedily found its way down to Mr Turner's desk, from whence I heard this mighty roar, 'MISS SOLOMON'. I was marched upstairs to the Director of Transportation's office and asked to explain myself. My days of being a civil servant were numbered and I was fortunate to quickly find a much better-paid job in the private sector.

Rory used the offer of help he had got from Enoch Powell and secured a job as a research assistant in Conservative Central Office. It wasn't as well-paid as mine but it was extremely interesting and was the ideal platform from which to pursue a career in politics, which

Rory wanted to do. Mr Powell had set up a somewhat secretive unit hidden away in a small office in the attic. The purpose of this unit was to better understand the adverse impacts that immigration was having in the country. Leading politicians in the party were largely in favour of encouraging immigration incorporating policies of assimilation to make up for shortages in the labour market. Powell diametrically opposed this view foretelling violence in the streets, loss of cultural identity and the creation of a new cohort of electors who would vote Labour and not Conservative. The former health minister, who had been sacked by Ted Heath after his Rivers of Blood speech, tasked Rory and a secretarial assistant to investigate and report back.

This was just the sort of intellectual and political challenge that Rory relished and, to my annoyance, he wouldn't stop talking about it at home. Rory explained how immigration had exploded since the end of the war. When hostilities ended Europe was awash with refugees and displaced persons; the first to arrive in England were about 120,000 Poles, who settled in large communities in Manchester, Bradford and west London. At the same time about 100,000 people from Ukraine and the Baltic States also came to the UK. Then the Windrush generation brought some 150,000 coloured people from the West Indies and by the time Rory started his job this number was increasing exponentially thanks to the birth of little black babies. There was an influx of Hungarians in 1956 after the Russian invasion. And not long after Rory started his job some 60,000 Asians, expelled from Uganda, arrived on these shores. They joined communities of other Asians from India and Pakistan who had been settling in the UK since the 1930s.

Rory, reading between the lines, assessed that what he was being asked to do was to provide Mr Powell with political ammunition in a climate dominated by controversial race relations legislation, the talk of new immigration laws and the fear of violence in the streets. There had been race riots in places like Notting Hill and Southall. Important though statistics were, Mr Powell said he needed evidence that shook people up and information that posed a threat to their way of life. Rory recalled some of the seminars he attended in Dundee where a new breed of sociologists were using interview techniques to gather what they called qualitative data. He put a case for some funding and was granted all the money he asked for. Rory interviewed some 200 people all over England and came up with some revealing insights and feedback that was political dynamite.

One respondent said, 'I don't want parts of my country to be no go areas, where I feel I can't walk for fear of being knifed or mugged. I don't want to be with black people. Why should I'?

Another said, 'it's a crime. First they all come here where they don't belong and they know it. Then they want their relatives and their relatives' relatives. And would you believe the government lets them have anything they wish'.

A mechanic from Croydon said, 'we've suffered enough. We've had one flabby government after another saying "we've got to live together". Well why? They don't have to live with them, killing goats, wailing in the morning, using our NHS and being a nuisance'.

The country was an unhappy place and Rory had also to factor in industrial strife, the three day week and the controversy over whether Britain should join the European Economic Community or not. The political situation came to a head when the Labour government decided to hold a referendum about membership of the EEC. The question on the ballot paper was, 'Do you think the United Kingdom should stay in the European Community (the Common Market)'?

Most members of the Labour government and the Conservative opposition favoured a 'yes 'vote. Those in the 'no' camp came from both ends of the political spectrum, making for unusual bedfellows, with Mr Powell on the right and Tony Benn on the far left. Rory was against joining Europe. He felt that by joining the Common Market we would lose our sovereignty and increase the risks of even higher levels of immigration. Rory sided with Mr Powell and was very active in the background, preparing campaign material, press statements and organising speaking engagements. Sadly for Powell he came out on the losing side but all was not lost because Rory had impressed some senior members of the party.

Chapter 18   Rory

1977 & The next few years - London

The result of the referendum was a disappointment but, on the bright side, Callaghan's government was very unpopular and our chances under our new leader, Margaret Thatcher, were looking good. My work during the referendum also generated a lot of praise and even though I was on the minority Eurosceptic wing of the party the top echelons in HQ said that I possessed abilities that the party should benefit from. I was given a good pay rise, and given more responsibility. I was moved from my isolated office in the attic to become part of the mainstream and given a bigger role in helping with the forthcoming general election. That proved to be a good career move. We won the election with Mrs Thatcher gaining a majority of 44 seats. Maggie, as we knew her at HQ, was the first woman to become PM and when she came round to Smith Square to thank the backroom staff she shook my hand and said, 'the party needs people like you'. When I got home and told Kathleen she said, 'I look forward to being an MP's wife. It is not appropriate to be a bidie-in so let's get married'. So, with a minimum of fuss, we made arrangements at the registry office in Lambeth Town Hall. It was a quiet affair with a friend each from work as our witnesses. We were very happy but a wee bit fearful about telling our parents.

We needn't have worried. Attitudes had changed significantly since the 1960s and both sets of parents were absolutely delighted. They both insisted we come up to the Borders as soon as possible. We were knocked out when we discovered both sets of parents had organised a massive ceilidh at the rugby club for all the family and our old friends. It was good to be back.

With Thatcher in power the country began to recover. There was a feel-good factor. Prince Charles married Diana Spencer in a massive media event of national euphoria. Thatcher, against all odds, threw the Argies out of the Falklands. Then she defeated the miners. On the international front the cold war was coming to an end and in 1989 the Berlin Wall fell. It was a good decade to be involved in politics. It was also a good time personally. I was making a reputation for myself as one of the party's experts on immigration.

Just after the end of the second Brixton race riot in 1985 - the first one had occurred in 1981 leading to an aftermath of simmering racial tension - there was a knock on my office door. I said, 'enter' and in walked the Duke of Cavers. I knew him as the chairman of the Roxburgh and Central Borders Conservative Association as well as the landlord of my father's farm on the Cavers Estate. The Duke, or Archie Scott as he preferred to be called, said, 'I'm in town to talk in this afternoon's debate in the Lords and I would like to take you to lunch'. I was surprised by his presence and flattered by the invitation. About half an hour later we climbed the steps of the RAC Club half way along Pall Mall between the Carlton Club and The Ritz. Archie was greeted by the concierge who took our hats and coats. We entered the drawing room and ordered gin and tonics. As I sank into a slightly worn, wingback, leather armchair I was struck by the pother of smoke with the aroma of Monte Cristo cigars perfuming the atmosphere.

'Look young Singer I understand you have become one of the party's leading experts on the scourge of immigration and the refugee problem. Bring me up to date'.

I thought this might be the reason for this unexpected lunch invitation and had been trying to sort out my thoughts as we walked over here through St James' Park. I began somewhat hesitantly, 'you will obviously be aware of the 1971 Immigration Act introduced largely as a result of the furore created by Mr Powell. The Act was designed to control the numbers of commonwealth immigrants but one of the unseen consequences of the referendum result is that it has opened the door to freer movement of workers from EEC countries. I am currently working on the statistics and cannot update you but I would suggest this is a problem waiting to happen. The act also restricted entry to holders of work permits or people who had parents or grand parents living in the UK. I would point out that one thing that is often overlooked is that the birthrate of immigrants was significantly higher than that of the English or Scottish population. This meant that the coloured population was rising at a faster rate than native whites. On the statistical front during the 1970s the average number of immigrants increasing the population was around 72,000 a year.

It is a wee bit lower now but because there are distinct settlement patterns where immigrants can outnumber locals such as Brixton, Notting Hill, Smethwick, Bradford and parts of Lancashire and West Yorkshire, racial tensions and pressure on local services such as health and schools have a disproportionate effect. One of the quirks I have recently been looking at is the increasing number of English people moving to live in Scotland. I can tell you that, looking at the 1971 and 1981 census results, the number of English people living in Scotland increased from around 279,000 to nearly 300,000. What these figures don't show, and this is another area we are researching, is that because there has been a downturn in the textile industry in the east Midlands and the north of England large cohorts of unemployed Asian textile workers have moved to Glasgow. Why there? We don't know'.

Archie Scott nodded and indicated he wanted me to to continue. 'What I can tell you is that significant numbers of immigrants are now living in our country. Mr Powell was right when he said this would increase the threat of violence. I think we can also say they are threatening our way of life, that ideas of assimilation are not working. And, they are definitely putting undue pressure on our already stretched health and education services'.

Archie said, 'you have been very thorough and helpful'. I interrupted, 'before I forget there is also the problem of refugees. So far we have only been talking about economic migrants. There are also refugees fleeing from war, torture, famine and worse'. After a pause for effect I continued, 'I am sure you will be aware that we are a signatory to the UN 1951 Refugee Convention as well as the 1967 Protocol. This means we have a responsibility to offer protection to people who seek asylum and fall into the legal definition of a "refugee", and moreover not to return or *refoule* any displaced person to places where they would otherwise face persecution'. I added, 'in this respect we have recently seen an influx of refugees escaping from the civil war in Somalia. I also understand there is intelligence suggesting there is trouble brewing in Burundi and between the Tutsis and Hutus in Rwanda'.

'Singer, you have been incredibly helpful and given me a most thorough briefing for the debate later this afternoon. I propose to raise the topics of managed migration and the development of a points based system controlling entry visas on the basis of need. I would like to kick around some of my ideas but we don't have time today. There is another matter that I would like to raise with you. As chairman of the Roxburgh and Central Borders Conservative Association I and other members of the management committee have been exploring ways we can loosen the grip Liberals have on the constituency. We have been taking a close look at your achievements at Central Office and would like to invite you up to the Borders to discuss the possibility of you becoming our candidate at the next election.

Chapter 19   Rory

1990-2 - The Scottish Borders

It was a fairly warm evening. We parked the car in Mart Street and walked along Bourtree Place. We were in our glad rags. I was wearing an Austin Reed double-breasted dark grey suit with a white shirt and blue silk tie. As it was a special occasion I was wearing my shiny Oxford patterned black shoes, made by Church's in Northampton. Kathleen was wearing a light blue Pringle's twin set made and designed in the nearby Glebe Mill. She was wearing a matching plaid tweed skirt, a pair of sensible shoes with low heels and carrying a Gucci handbag I had splashed out on for this occasion. We climbed up six steps and entered the double doors of the Con Club, glancing up at the frieze bearing the inscription: 'MEMORIAL STONE LAID BY MARGARET COUNTESS OF DALKEITH 16TH OCTOBER 1897'. Entering the central lobby, with its parquet floor, we saw a bar to the right and a snooker room to the rear. We knew we were expected to go up the wide mahogany stairs to be interviewed by the candidate selection panel of the local Conservative association. We were both nervous and felt the eyes of Margaret Thatcher trying to pierce our souls from a large framed print of her official portrait painted by Rodrigo Moynihan.

We knocked on the large door, also mahogany. 'Come in'. I recognised the voice of the Duke of Cavers.

194

'Sit yourselves down'. We sat on two chairs in front of a long table with the Duke and five members of his committee sitting on the other side. I recognised everyone. There was Mr Hogg the butcher, Sandy Aitchison provost of Galashiels, Ross Douglas the finance director of Tarbert Knitwear, Mr Haynes a local solicitor and Mrs Macintosh the wife of the wee free minister in Selkirk. The Duke started off by asking me to speak for no more than five minutes to introduce myself, where I came from, my family background, education, employment history, political experience and why I thought I could defeat the sitting Liberal. Before I started he said, 'I know that is a tall order for just five minutes but that is all the time Mr Speaker is likely to give you in an adjournment debate in the House of Commons. It will show us your metal, after which my colleagues and I will ask you and Mrs Singer some questions'.

The five minutes went by in a flash. I thought I had acquitted myself fairly well. I had done my homework and had prepared answers to questions I thought I might be asked. That proved to be a good move. Mr Haynes the solicitor, asked me several technical questions about the drafting of legislation. His questions did not cause me any bother because of some of the work I had done at Central Office. I think I created a good impression. Next up was Mr Hogg. As well as being a butcher he was a high heid yin on the local chamber of commerce. He was concerned about the corrosive impact of immigration. His interest surprised me as the only black faces in Hawick were a handful of immigrants who were nurses at the Cottage Hospital. As with Mr Haynes I think my specialist knowledge impressed him too. The first political questioning came from the Tarbert finance director. He was a Eurosceptic and his business faced stiff competition from Italian knitwear companies like Pisano and Colours of Benetton. I wasn't too sure about competition in the textile trade but I hope I had impressed him with the story of the background paper I had prepared for Mrs Thatcher about objecting to the single currency. Then came the Gala Provost. He gave me some cause for concern arising from his follow up questions to my response to his first question.

Mr Aitchison started by asking, 'where were you born'? I replied, 'Ottawa, Ontario in Canada. My father, who had been born here, was at the time working in the British High Commission after serving as a Royal Airforce Officer in…'. Mr Aitchison cut me off and said, 'that's it then. You were born abroad. What passport do you hold'? I said, 'Canadian. Ever since my parents brought me back to the UK I haven't travelled abroad so I have had no need to apply for a British passport'. Mr Aitchison said, 'that doesn't matter a damn. You are foreign and you don't have a British passport. You cannot become a member of our parliament'. At this the Duke intervened and said, 'I am sure that commonwealth citizens are treated the same as British citizens'. That seemed to take a bit of sting out of the provost's attack. I then decided to bullshit and talk about something I wasn't sure of. 'I think Mr Aitchison if you look at the second part of the 1981 British Nationality Act that you will find that his Grace is right. That seemed to ameliorate Mr Aitchison and the Duke said, 'over to you Mrs Macintosh'.

'I would like to ask Mrs Singer some questions. It is so important to make sure that our MP's spouse is a woman of the highest integrity. Mrs Singer, welcome. Can you tell me how many children you have and are they boys or girls and do they go to Sunday School'? Kathleen answered, 'none. I am afraid we have none. It's the way things have turned out'. 'That's a shame', sniped Mrs Macintosh. I was sure she didn't mean that it was a shame we were childless after trying for years but that it was a shame we would not present the image of the perfect family. Mrs Macintosh was a bit of a harridan as well as a bigot. Her next question was, 'you're a Jewess aren't you'? I could see Kathleen bristling. She held fire, as if inviting me to comment, but before I could Kathleen forcefully said, 'that is a totally irrelevant question and I don't care if what I am about to say damages my husband's chances of selection but I am sure he will agree your anti-semitic attitude is wholly out of place in a modern Conservative Party and I think you should offer your resignation or be fired from this committee'. I secretly admired what Kathleen said and the vehement manner in which she said what she did. The Duke intervened and said, 'I don't think we need to go there just now. Mr and Mrs Singer thank you for coming along this evening. If you would care to go downstairs to the bar and have a coffee or a drink we will let you know our decision before you go home'.

We both ordered a double whisky and spent the next very long half hour waiting to hear our fate. There was a glass door between the bar, the lobby and staircase and the first movement we saw was Mrs Macintosh coming down the stairs fastening up her coat. Five minutes later the Duke and his colleagues entered the bar. Mr Hogg went straight over to the barman and ordered a bottle of champagne and seven glasses. A smiling Duke came over to our table and said, 'congratulations, we would like you to be our PPC'.

That announcement brought about a material change in our life style. We had to find a house in the constituency. In the short term we moved into the granny flat which had been added to the big old house the Solomons had recently bought in the neighbouring village of Denholm. We moved in there on a temporary basis.

Our lives changed significantly. We both had to continue to earn a living and even with the financial help we received from an anonymous donor we had to carry on working in London. Politically this was advantageous. It was easy to keep in touch with important members of the party as well as being able to smooze with journalists from Fleet Street, radio and television. The weekends were a flurry of activity - listening to the concerns and issues raised by the membership and showing our faces round the constituency. In the winter this involved going to rugby matches and in the summer being seen around at common ridings, Gala's braw lads events, Kelso Civic Week and the Jethart Festival. I also attended a wide range of functions from Rotary, to Probus and old folks' coffee mornings.

I was most fortunate in inheriting a very experienced agent, George Foulkes. George was a wise old cove who knew everybody you needed to know locally. He also had an amazing range of contacts in the party nationally. It was a conversation he had had with the organisers of the party conference that gave me the platform to make a name for myself. The 1991 conference was held in Blackpool. We were coming to the end of the parliamentary term and an election was not far off. After years in government and the loss of Margaret Thatcher as our leader meant the press and polls showed that it was going to be a close run thing between Major and Kinnock.

One weekend in August George took me aside in the Con Club bar and counselled that now I had created a positive awareness of who I was and what I stood for in the constituency it was the time to begin to get noticed nationally. He said that in certain circles of the party I was highly respected for my knowledge of and stance on immigration. George felt that this put me in good stead with the right wing of the party after what the wets had done to Thatcher. He said he could get me in as a speaker at one of the Fringe meetings. His advice was to curry favour with the right by talking about my relationship with Enoch Powell and how I had worked with him in the background from my days as an undergraduate through to my experience of central office. George said I should capitalise on the audience's fears that the British way of life was under attack. I said that all this had been said before and that this was nothing new. George said,'repeat, repeat, repeat. If you want to be heard you need to repeat, repeat, repeat. Stay with the same message but ram it home by giving example after example. Let me tell you; Powell talked of "Rivers of Blood"; in the past few years we have had example after example - in Brixton, Toxteth, Handsworth, South Shields. I could go on and on'.

'Okay, I've got the point', I interrupted him. 'But I have got to say something new and I think I know what will strike a chord - a new threat from an uncontrolled flow of refugees and illegal immigrants. Over the last couple of years I had noticed that refugees were coming into the country in ever increasing numbers. This was a trend that I had been taking a close look at but not saying anything publicly about it. I thought here was my chance. I had noticed that since the fall of the Berlin Wall there had been an increase of some 20,000 refugees and that this number appeared to be increasing exponentially. Other trouble spots around the world were also creating instability and people were fleeing for their lives and likely to create an influx of refugees from the likes of Yugoslavia, Somalia and Rwanda. Over the next few weeks I drafted and redrafted my speech and rehearsed it *ad nauseam*. The big day came. My conference debut created a lot of noise generating headlines in the broadsheets and tabloids. '*Firebrand lights up the Fringe, Singer's Warning Song about Refugees*, and *Singer in Tune with Powell*.

Chapter 20   Kathleen

1994 - The Scottish Borders & Stobs Camp

Shortly after Rory was elected as a member of parliament I gave up my job in London and moved permanently into our flat in Denholm. Rory kept on the flat in de Laune Street as it was very convenient for the House. The young doctors who had shared the London house were now consultants and had long gone. Rory shared the house now with two elderly spinsters who were no threat - I was aware what politicians got up to when they were away from home. The ladies were also quiet and were fastidious about cleanliness and house keeping. It was the ideal arrangement. I effectively became Rory's secretary and assistant. It was a paid job - the money was useful as an MP's remuneration wasn't particularly generous. I was heavily involved with the minutiae of constituency work. It was quite challenging on occasions and it could be very rewarding when you helped get a constituent out of a hole. Every day was different. I was very busy helping Rory provide constituents with help on a range of problems from schooling, to benefits, pensions, housing, tax and the closure of rural bus services. In addition to sorting out Rory's constituency diary I got involved with a local campaign group to bring back the Waverley Line, which had been closed by Dr Beeching. Always near the top of the list was engaging with management and unions in the textile industry. Hawick in particular suffered from a downturn in demand and many thousands were laid off as mill after mill closed. As Tories we would normally side with management but having gained inside information we could see that some of the problems arose from very bad management decisions. One chief executive, Malcolm Brough, who we knew through his involvement in the local association, all of a sudden shut up shop and made 80 long-term employees redundant. Brough, who was a bit of a drinker, won a very large order for several dozen crew neck, lambswool jumpers in various sizes and colours, at a trade fair in Brussels. On returning to Hawick he placed a works order for the wool and set out a production schedule. The delivery time was short and he had to pay over-time rates to satisfy the customer's requirements. Everything was done on time. The day after delivery a very angry Belgian customer was on the phone saying that he was returning the order as Brough had delivered V necks and not the specified crew necks. Brough was not able to find another purchaser for the stock and the bank refused a loan to pay for the raw material and mill workers' wages. The company went into receivership.

Rory told me far worse stories about the goings on in the knitwear business where companies were laying off staff at an alarming rate. The rot had set in after the war when the widespread introduction of artificial fibres and lower production costs overseas led to a reduction in demand for woollen garments from Hawick. To make matters worse a 12-week-long strike for higher pay put the companies under a lot of strain. The strike was led by a communist firebrand and arch feminist, Maisie Hogg. Rumour had it, and Hawick was a community rife with gossip, that Maisie was Rory's secret mistress. One evening after too much chardonnay I tackled Rory, asking him if there was any truth in the rumours. To his credit, and my hurt, Rory was remarkably frank. He recalled that when he was thinking about becoming a PPC that he had gone to great lengths to meet the movers and shakers in the constituency. Maisie was a feisty young woman building a reputation as an influential shop steward in the Union of Women Mill Workers, the UWMW. Rory admitted to being flattered and taken in by this flirtatious young woman. One thing led to another.

The 12 week strike was eventually won by the women and the employers ended up having to pay wages that many struggled to meet. During the strike Maisie built a reputation for herself as a powerful and imaginative female trade union leader. She set up food kitchens in the High Street to feed hungry, striking families but her *pièce de resistance* was two simultaneous publicity stunts that got her on to the front pages and the nation's television screens. Her first initiative was to replace all the Hawick signs on the main roads at the entrance to the town with the words Dawson City to mock Dawson Corporation, the company that owned the largest knitwear company in the town. At the same time groups of UWMW strikers strung up effigies of Dawson directors from lampposts along the High Street. At midday in front of press and television cameras, in a gesture of gendered humiliation, Maisie burned the effigy outside the Town Hall.

But Rory had more to confess. He said, 'remember when I didn't come home for a couple of nights during the run up to the general election? Well I wasn't in London. I was kidnapped by Maisie and five of the members of her sisterhood coven. They jumped me one evening when I came out of the Con Club. A damp kitchen towel with a sweet minty odour was placed over my mouth and nose - it was chloroform. I was out like a light and the next thing I knew I was lying tied down by four-ply cashmere wool on a shiny new Shima knitting machine. The mechanical parts were digging into my back and then I noticed I was only wearing my Lyle and Scott Y-Fronts. I was surrounded by six women who chanted slogans one after the other: "Some women fear the fire. Some women simply become it. . . Feminism isn't about making women strong. Women are already strong. . . Equal rights are not special rights. . . A woman's place is in the house - the House of Commons". Maisie interrupted and said, "he's coming round. It's time sisters". She paused for effect. "After three. One, two, three". In unison, like a well-drilled corps of squaddies, they all took off their blouses and T-shirts before unfastening their bras and piling them on the floor for Maisie to set fire to them with a Swan Vesta match. Kendra, Maisie's, number two, had a large pair of pinking shears in her hand. She approached me and before I knew it she had cut through my Y-Fronts, removed them and threw them on top of the small bonfire of burning bras on the factory floor. She grinned and said, "that's what Joan of Arc and hundreds of falsely convicted witches had to put up with. Power to the sisterhood"! She bent down and brought a lipstick out of her hand bag. The other women did the same. Maisie said, "Kendra you go first". With a salacious grin on her face Kendra used her lipstick to scrawl a slogan on my chest. She was followed, one by one, by the others scrawling slogans, some short, some longer on my arms and thighs. I was terrified and at the same time excited and I fear it showed. Maisie was last to write. She filled the space at the bottom of my stomach resting her left hand on my exposed pubic hair. Kendra shrieked, "look girls we have to extinguish his manhood". Nodding her head she grabbed a fire extinguisher and covered my swelling in foam. That was the last I remembered until I woke up in Maisie's bathroom in her Burnfoot council house'.

Rory continued, 'I am really, really sorry I am telling you all this but if I am going to save our relationship and marriage I think I need to be honest with you'. He paused and I drew breath. 'The last time I had been in Maisie's bathroom had been two weeks before when she was showing me her brand new avocado bathroom suite and one of the first bidets to be installed in Hawick. This evening she was sitting on the bidet, fully clothed, with her bra-less nipples showing, erect, through her T-shirt. She had a nail brush in her hands. I was naked in the bath in four inches of warm water. What are you going to do with that? She replied, "I am going to scrub off all the lipstick slogans and see what happens next". I thought that was going to be painful but I had the presence of mind to ask her to tell me what the slogans said before the evidence was scrubbed off. She recited five mantras in common use by women's libbers and proudly told me she had written EQUAL PAY. I asked her what she meant by that. She wouldn't answer but I could tell by the lusty expression on her face that she had regretted what had happened during the evening and wanted to make up with me in her bedroom next door'.

'I am really, really sorry Kathleen but sadly all that is true. I feel I owe you the truth before the epidemic of gossip and innuendo that beset this town become rumours that get distorted by time and embellished in the retelling'. I was totally gob smacked and was rendered speechless. There was a long uncomfortable silence between us. Rory, ever the politician, could not stay silent for long and tried to rescue the situation. 'I am reluctant to say this but perhaps some good will come out of my shame. You know that they say that women usually wheedle secrets out of men through pillow talk. In my case I think the roles have been reversed. When I asked Maisie again what she meant by EQUAL PAY she told me that a clause in Barbara Castle's Equal Pay Act meant that women had to receive equal pay for the same or equivalent work carried out by men and that she was planning a major strike later in the year'.

'I shared the salient bits of information with Ross Douglas, you remember from the selection panel. As well as being a high heid yin in the local party and finance director of Tarbert Knitwear he was chairman of the Hawick Textile Manufacturers Confederation. He told me to go away and find out more about the UWMW's tactics and consider strategies to defeat them. Well as sure as eggs were eggs, less than a month after my election, all Hawick textile companies were threatened with strike action unless women were granted equal pay with men. Ever since John Hardie had introduced the first knitting frame in Hawick at the end of the eighteenth century male frame workers were the top dogs in knitwear. In the early days male strength was needed to set up and work the frames. The frame workers gained status which they enhanced by forming an exclusive group with the know-how to set up the machines to knit simple and more elaborate patterns. Female workers were relegated to what were considered more menial tasks like collar linking, button-holing and greasy mending. They were paid at much lower rates than the male frame workers who, after the management and owners, were the dominant force in the mills. It was this traditional gender imbalance, which ironically created some unusual alliances, that Maisie and her co-workers were challenging'.

'The substance of Maisie's claim was that the traditional skills of frame workers were no longer required. Around the time of the strike, knitwear companies were introducing new technologies to replace the relative inefficiency of traditional frames. A Japanese company had developed automated Shima knitting machines that used computers and punched paper tape to control the knitting of different garments and patterns. This improved performance, lowered costs and improved quality without the need for the outdated skill set of the frame workers. In spite of this the frame workers, using their traditional strength, position and influence, maintained their wage differential. The UWMW considered this was unjust. They claimed that now frame workers were employed doing less skilled jobs as machine minders that the equal pay act meant female workers should be paid the same rate as the men. Under the terms of the Barbara Castle Equal Pay Act women should be paid the same rate for the same or equivalent work as the men. After a lot of brain scratching I realised that this could be the weak link of the UWMW's case'.

After Rory's long explanation I was slowly becoming more amenable to forgiving him or at least understanding that his infidelity could be turned to our mutual advantage. Shortly after Rory's electoral success I took a call from Ross Douglas in our Denholm flat. Mr Douglas wanted Rory to come to a breakfast meeting at his home the following morning. Rory was the first to arrive at Mr Ross' home, Invercraik, a large rambling former hunting lodge a couple of miles from Roberton. Invercraik was full of antique furniture and Scottish paintings by the likes of Anne Redpath, Willian Gillies and Glasgow artists from the Spook School, whose elongated figures and elaborate distortions of form were thought eccentric and even macabre by some of their contemporaries. Rory was ushered into the dining room where there was a long mahogany table set for eight. There was a matching side table with a hot plate offering a choice of kippers, scrambled egg with smoked salmon, tattie scones alongside a bowl of pink grapefruit segments and red cubes of watermelon in a basin of crushed ice. Rory explained, 'before I could sit down four cars arrived one after the other. I knew all of the arrivals but was astonished by their composition. Five of the guests were directors of different knitwear companies and members of the Hawick Textile Manufacturing Confederation. The sixth was Jimmy McCartney, the controversial leader of the Frame Workers Union and your childhood school friend. What was he doing at this gathering? It quickly transpired that all the guests, other than me, were members of the Lodge. It was in everybody's interest to maintain the status quo and retain the gendered pecking order'.

By this stage I was gripped and nodded to Rory to go on. 'Ross Douglas sat on a Chippendale carver, at the head of the table. He began by saying that we all knew why we were here. He mentioned that our new member of parliament had a possible solution to the current problem. Mr Ross asked me to take the floor. I told the assembled company that I had looked at the Equal Pay Act in great detail. I explained that by law, men and women must get equal pay for doing equal work. This is work that the equal pay law classes as the same, similar, equivalent or of equal value. My solution was that all we had to do was to prove that the work of the women was not equivalent to the work of the frame workers. I suggested that we should offer the UWMW an independent review of what work was equivalent and what work was not. I told those present that I had had confidential discussions with the constituency party chairman's brother who was the senior partner in a firm of international accountants and management consultants. Davidson, Ogilvy, Simpson, Harvey, known as DOSH, was a highly respected firm who I was sure the UWMW would respect as an independent arbiter to settle the dispute. Unknown to the bra-burning trade unionists I had negotiated a deal with DOSH that, for a substantial fee which would cost less than an unfavourable wage increase, they would conclude that female jobs were not equivalent. Those around the table accepted my proposition and then the UWMW agreed to this method of arbitration. This move ultimately led to the female workers accepting the status quo. As far as I was concerned my stock rose to new heights in the upper echelons of the party at Westminster as well as in the Borders'.

* * *

While presenting a more public face to his constituents Rory retained his interest in immigration and refugees. Such was his reputation that he was given an unpaid advisory role at the Home Office. Much of Rory's time was spent researching and tracking the data to predict new trends and identify potential problem areas. When he spoke at the Fringe meeting at Blackpool Rory mentioned he thought that Rwanda could be the source of a new influx of refugees. His forecast was tellingly prescient. Trouble between the Tutsis and Hutus led to a level of violence rarely experienced before. In a three month period there had been a massive killing spree with reports of between half a million and a million being killed. This genocide created a massive outflow of refugees. Initially this was not a problem in the UK because most of the refugees ended up in neighbouring countries. Additionally, relatively large numbers travelled on to the Cherbourg peninsula in the north of France. The French authorities, who were fairly authoritarian, were not happy and made life very difficult for the refugees. This official attitude played into the hands of people smugglers who, for large sums of money, found there was a ready demand from the refugees to be smuggled on small boats to the Channel Islands. Between August and September hundreds of boats smuggled thousands of refugees from the Plage de Denneville to the beaches of Grouville in Jersey. Jersey, though the largest of the Channel Islands, is only nine miles long and five miles wide and soon became inundated. The States of Jersey and the Home Office agreed that surplus numbers would be transferred by ferry to hotels on the south coast of England. The problem was that refugees from Rwanda kept on coming. Costs of providing hotel accommodation rocketed, violence erupted and the prophecies of Enoch Powell well and truly came to pass. The government and the Home Office were in a bind. They were obliged under international law to deal sympathetically with refugees but their presence was very unpopular from Kent to Dorset and further afield. Lots of brains in the Home Office were set to find a solution. Rory was asked by the Home Secretary not to be timid but to be radical and to think outside the box.

The Friday after he was asked to do this Rory and I, along with a couple of bottles of wine and a picnic hamper, took ourselves off to the isolated banks of St Mary's Loch to see what ideas we could come up with. This picnic took me back to Arthurstone Terrace when Lorna, Mark, Rory and I would put the world to rights and talk a lot of rubbish. The location of St Mary's Loch was a more stimulating environment. Rory and I had some mad ideas and some that were so different that they might work. We rabbited on about sending an armed UN task force to Rwanda to bash a few heads together. Then we considered a massive aid package to bring the country together by hosting the 2000 Olympic Games. At a more practical level we thought about paying the French police to stop the refugees embarking from Normandy beaches and to turn the boats back if they could get offshore. 'I know', said Rory, 'we should call this "Project Row Back the Boats"'. Another idea, which appeared to have traction, was to create internment camps in the UK for the refugees. This initiative would massively reduce the costs of hotel accommodation. It would also separate the refugees from the local population and we could make it such an unpleasant environment that it would act as a deterrent. We both liked this idea and kicked it round and round the houses. We didn't notice it getting dark, but we did notice a drop in the temperature and the irritation of being bitten by midges. We headed off to Tibbie Shiels Inn at the end of the loch. There was a spare guest room available so we had supper and stayed the night. We were feeling good, if not a little itchy.

When Rory returned to London he told the Home Secretary about our idea for internment camps. The Home Secretary thought it was an excellent idea and told Rory to go away and identify some potential locations and produce a feasibility study. Rory was particularly busy at that time preparing for the party conference and rushing through a couple of troublesome bills so he asked me to come up with a plan.

This was something to get my teeth into. There was one obvious location for a refugee internment camp. I jumped in the car and took the Newcastleton road out of Hawick. I turned right after the pig farm and after going up the narrow winding road I stopped the car at the top of the hill. A steep valley in the middle of nowhere lay before me. On the hill in front I could see the layout of the roads that wound round the former Stobs camp and in between the brick foundations of the hundred or so huts that had accommodated some 6,000 former PoWs and internees. The MoD had sold off the huts to local farmers, a scout troop and nursery schools after the war. The roads were a little overgrown and covered in sheep shit but I could see that the infrastructure to supply water and power was largely in place. The foundations for the mess hall, kitchens, bakery and hospital were all intact and would provide the perfect footprint for temporary replacement structures. Most importantly the perimeter fence was largely intact though one or two sections would need replacing. Above all Stobs was isolated. In winter it was a godforsaken hole and totally fulfilled the brief to create a strong deterrent effect.

The land was part of the Cavers' Estate. One phone call to the factor was all that it took to get permission to recreate Stobs Camp to house refugees. I also talked to a timber company in Jedburgh who quickly came through with plans to build temporary wooden huts. They even came up with the idea to create three-tier bunks like those in submarines to fit in more refugees, so saving money and making the experience of living there even more miserable. I achieved a lot in that first week and when Rory arrived home he was absolutely delighted and announced that recreating Stobs was a "stonking" idea. What delighted him most was that having had family from both sides spending years of their lives inside the fence he kept on saying how much he looked forward to being the first Singer looking in from the outside.

The political situation was tricky with a number of issues, over and above the refugee crisis, creating problems for the government. Downing Street was concerned that with two by-elections coming up along the south coast they risked reducing their already small majority. Rory was conscious of these threats to the party. Because of this he knew that the Home Secretary was likely to give the go ahead to rebuild Stobs for Rwandan Refugees. What surprised Rory was that the Home Secretary said that Rory's plan to have the first refugees arriving in three months was too long. He ordered that the first huts must be ready in eight weeks.

The next period of our lives was more hectic than we could have imagined. We had to find suppliers, negotiate contracts, start construction, sort out bills of quantities, recruit a highly competent clerk of works, organise the catering arrangements, sort out electricity, water and sewerage while at the same time recruiting and training camp guards. How we did it I don't know and the big day arrived. The press office had done us proud. Ranks of photographers, television cameramen and journalists with pencils and notepads were lined up for the official opening ceremony. Rory was given the honour of introducing the Home Secretary and thanking the legion of people who had worked above and beyond. The Home Secretary gave a speech talking about the problems of immigration and refugees, and how Stobs Refugee Camp was a cost effective solution and a critical part of the government's "row back the boats"policy. Seconds after he cut the ribbon in front of the gate the first green SMT bus, carrying refugees, pulled up in front of the guard house. The first bedraggled set of refugees trooped off and gave their names when asked. They were all black but the last group off was a white man, about my age, with a woman and two children.. The guard said, 'name'. The refugee answered, 'Hersinger'. Rory gasped and lent over to whisper in my ear, 'I think that's my second cousin'!

Afterword

Dear Reader,

As this is my first venture into writing fiction I thought you might appreciate knowing where I was coming from.

In 2023 I sat down nearly every day in front of my keyboard to write my third book, *Voices of Hawick Rugby*. I had no complaints. This was a labour of love. The manuscript was based on oral history recordings and personal testimonies from some 200 people. I was working to a deadline and had to be disciplined. The book had to be published on time to coincide with the 150th anniversary of the Hawick Rugby Club. My nine to five regime was most enjoyable and when it came to an end I was lost. How was I going to fill my days? I had become addicted to writing.

I soon realised that, as a retired person, this was the ideal opportunity to fulfil a long-held ambition to write a novel. Before writing the *Voices of Hawick Rugby*, I had previously published two academic books, also based on oral history testimonies, about the experiences of immigrants in Scotland and Canada. In another project I had also carried out oral history interviews with some 60 people who had experienced the trauma of deindustrialisation and the decline of the textile industry. I reasoned that all this experience and knowledge would provide excellent sources of information for novel writing.

Oral historians generally adopt one of two approaches, either through interviews based on a questionnaire or through a few open-ended questions. The latter approach encourages the interviewee to tell you what they think, free from providing answers they think the interviewer wants to hear. I have always followed the open-ended approach as this tends to provide reminiscences that provide a more textured recall of the ups and downs of human life . . . what emotions people experienced, what was life like before the internet, what was it like to live without central heating or modern appliances, what did the world smell like, what sounds could you hear, how did people live, what friendships did they have? . . . indeed a treasure trove of information to bring an enhanced sense of reality and insight to historical fiction writing.

As an historian I have gone to great lengths to base my story on the realities of historical, human experience. I believe it important to help the reader appreciate the realities of life in days gone by. In the main I have sought to reflect these realities and the flavour of life related to the time periods being described. I do occasionally make reference to actual characters such as Camillien Houde and Enoch Powell. I have sought to write about these characters with historical accuracy but there is a deliberate blurring of facts when they engage with fictional characters in the narrative. For example, Camillien Houde did not have a brother called Claudio. Enoch Powell's relationship with Rory Singer is entirely fictional but, arguably, it is not out of character.

Writing fiction is completely different from writing an historical monograph where precision, accuracy and the provision of corroboration along with detailed citation of evidence is a must. When one is writing about fact, in an academic book, the author has to keep detailed records to provide accurate citations providing precise data where the information was found so that readers can check the primary or secondary sources referred to. What this means is that the author must always know what the facts are. In writing fiction, other than much less rigorous notes and the fallibilities of memory, the author does not have access to such precise information. As a consequence I often forgot what happened earlier in the narrative. This can have disastrous consequences. For example I forgot the Christian name of the Carlucci's son. I started off calling him Pietro and months later, when I was further into writing the book, Pietro had inexplicably morphed into Roberto. I can tell you that rigorous copy editing spotted that blunder. I fear there may be other unintentional inconsistencies and my apologies if there are. If you spot any do let me know and you will be in line to win a copy of the sequel, *Under Pressure of Time*.

I have already mentioned that the hundreds of oral history interviews I have recorded over the last twenty or so years have been invaluable in helping the narrative come to life. Let me give you one example. I wanted to show how cold winters were for shepherds in the 1930s, before the days of quad bikes and modern fabrics that provided thermal insulation and waterproofing. In an oral history interview, held in the Scottish Borders Memory Bank, an elderly shepherd recalled how he would come in from a day in the snow, take off his tweed coat and stand it, frozen solid, in front of a coal fire until it melted in a heap in time to dry out ready for use in the morning.

Personal memory, though not always reliable, was also an important source for me when I was writing about places and events in the past. For example the primary school in the first chapter bears an uncanny resemblance to my days at the old St Mary's School at the top of Café Brae in Hawick. Not all the events described there actually happened but some did, like lying down on the railway line and getting into trouble at home. Similarly, time spent in Canada, when I taught at Carleton University in Ottawa proved very helpful in adding authenticity to my descriptions of Ontario and New Brunswick. Indeed, I can tell you that the account of the British High Commissioner's residence, Earnscliffe, was based on my having lunch there when I was asked to give a talk about my earlier book, *Invisible Immigrants: The English in Canada since 1945*.

Primary and secondary sources were also essential. In particular my descriptions of British concentration camps in south Africa during the Boer War relied on official materials and database compilations published by the Department of Historical Studies, University of Cape Town. Contemporary novels by authors like John Buchan and Henry Rider Haggard helped me add and recreate local colour. Documentary sources were also helpful in the Canadian chapters. In this respect I was fortunate to possess the private papers and log book of my father, F/Sgt A.M. Watson. Dad was a flying instructor during World War II in, amongst other places, Moncton, New Brunswick.

Covering the interwar years through to where my story ends in the 1990s I benefitted from the work of a number of social and political historians. The following books proved particularly valuable: David Kynaston's *Austerity Britain: 1945-51*, *Family Britain: 1951-57* and *A Northern Wind: Britain 1962-65*; Arthur Marwick's, *British Society since 1945*; David Kirby's, *1947 Britain: Hope amongst Hardship*; TC Smout's, *Century of the Scottish People: 1830-1950*; and JM Bumstead's, *The Peoples of Canada: A Post-Confederation History*.

I continue to marvel how earlier novelists coped without the internet. When I wanted to check a fact or find out information my ever-reliable search engine provided the answers instantly. In chapter ten I initially wrote that the badge of an RCMP Mountie had a horse's head at its centre. When rereading this description some weeks later I thought this sounded too good to be true so checked it out on the Internet. Up came lots of images of the badge showing a bison in the centre!

Technology aside, so many people helped with *Distorted in Time's* creation. I am fortunate to live where I do just over the hill from Stobs Camp. I live amongst the sheep farmers of Teviotdale and am indebted to Walter and Pat Douglas for ensuring the authenticity of my description of the lifestyle of a shepherd in the 1930s. Walter also told me that he knew of a former German, Stobs PoW who remained as a farm labourer after the Great War and who, just like my character Gërnot/Gerald, anglicised his name. Pat also read and commented on the manuscript as did others. Worthy of thanks for their input and help are Fiona Benton, Suzann Tomlinson, Ken Bogle, Professor Douglas Scott, Jules Horne and members of the Upper Teviotdale Pastoral Society Wine and Chocolate Book Club. Thanks are due to Hannah and Peter Gee for their photographs of Stobs Camp. Last, but certainly not least, there is my wife, Maggie. Not only did she not complain when I was sitting at my keyboard when I should have been outside cutting the grass but she was an incredibly supportive and constructive critic as well as being a pernickety copy checker and grammarian. During her first read through I heard her audibly gasp when she reached the end of the story. I wonder if you shared her surprise?

I do read a lot, both fiction and factual books. One of my occasional frustrations is there is usually very little information about the authors. So, in this case, I would like to put that right. Here is a little background information. I live with my wife of 53 plus years in the Scottish Borders, just over the hill from Stobs Camp. In 1987 I founded a marketing consultancy company from a shed in my garden in Hampshire - that company is now an international award-winning enterprise with offices in Europe, the USA, Australia, the Middle and Far East. I retired early and gained a PhD studying the effects of English immigration to Scotland. I became an Honorary Research Fellow at the University of Dundee and had spells as a visiting academic at Carleton

University in Ottawa. I have published three books and have spoken at the Edinburgh International and Borders Book Festivals as well as appearing occasionally on television and radio.

Finally, I would like to say that this book is a genuine work of fiction with occasional passing references to real historical characters. They are only there to add veracity to the story. I hope you enjoyed reading *Distorted by Time* at least half as much as I enjoyed writing it.

I am also grateful for the professionalism and consistently high standards delivered by Julie Scott and her colleagues at Grosvenor House Publishing.

Murray Watson
Teviotdale, Winter 2025.

About the Font

The text of *Distorted by Time* is reproduced in Palatino. I chose this font not just because it is elegant and easy to read but because it is a metaphor for one of the themes in my story. Palatino was designed by the German typographer, Herman Zapf, at the end of World War II. Through its design Zapf wanted to create a new German identity moving away from the image and identity created by heavy Germanic typefaces that typified Imperial and Nazi Germany. For similar motives Gërnot Hersinger wanted to deconstruct and then reconstruct his identity as Gerald Singer.